Tough Justice

Burt Lowell has been living as a recluse in an abandoned ghost town but someone puts a price on his head, and he wants to find out who, and why.

Confronted by a gang of gunslicks, the trail leads to Rickard, a scheming ranch owner, but there is a more sinister figure behind him, the elusive railroad boss, Mossman. Riding for the rival Long Rail brand, Lowell sets off on a trail drive to Shoshone Flats where Mossman has opened a branch line. But where is he? The search for the truth becomes a quest for revenge. Somewhere down the tracks Lowell must find and confront Mossman on his own ground if he is to arrive at a final resolution.

Tough Justice

Colin Bainbridge

A Black Horse Western

ROBERT HALE · LONDON

© Colin Bainbridge 2014
First published in Great Britain 2014

ISBN 978-0-7198-1357-3

Robert Hale Limited
Clerkenwell House
Clerkenwell Green
London EC1R 0HT

www.halebooks.com

Typeset by
Derek Doyle & Associates, Shaw Heath
Printed and bound in Great Britain by
CPI Antony Rowe, Chippenham and Eastbourne

CHAPTER ONE

Abbot Mossman wasn't the sort of man to spend any time in town, although he was reputed to own a good part of Shoshone Flats. He had certainly acquired the railroad line and stood to make a lot of money shipping cattle. He was known to be a recluse. Nobody knew for certain where he lived or even what he looked like. Rumours circulated about him but he was elusive and escaped definition. So it would have come as something of a shock to the telegraph operator if he had known that the tall, stooping figure with the lank white hair who entered his office was none other than Mossman himself. This fact alone indicated the importance Mossman attached to the message he sent, addressed to Ludwig Rickard, business man and rancher in the town of Granton. It read simply:

Deal with Burt Lowell.

When he had finished, Mossman walked out of the telegraph office and began to make his way towards the railroad station. He felt he could rely on Rickard to carry out his barely coded instruction. It was a minor matter but it needed to be dealt with quickly. He had thought Lowell was dead, burned to ashes in the fire he had started – the fire which had burned down a whole section of Buckhorn and set the seal on his plans for the stagecoach route. Only one other person knew about that: the lawyer, Dinsdale. There was nothing to fear from him, however, because he had been actively involved in the whole plot. It was all a long time ago; the whole affair was virtually forgotten. Then word had reached him that Lowell was still around and living, after a fashion, in the ruins of Buckhorn which was nothing now but a ghost town. Although Lowell represented a slim threat to his growing empire, he wasn't prepared to take any chances. Lowell had to die, and this time for good.

Burt Lowell opened his eyes and looked out from the balcony of the dilapidated hotel on the empty street below him. He had fallen asleep in his cane chair. It was still dark but he needed to get on the trail early if he was to collect his supplies and be back in Buckhorn by nightfall. Getting to his feet, he descended the outside staircase and entered the bar through the broken batwings. He brewed some coffee and then made his way towards the livery stable where he kept his horse. He whispered gently to it as he led it outside and hitched it to an old buckboard. Climbing up to the driver's seat, he took the reins.

At his prompting the horse stepped forward and the wagon began to move down the deserted street. On either side the frail clapboard buildings leaned together at odd angles, like old women at the pump, forming an indeterminate, almost immaterial mass in the pale moonlight. Some parts seemed to shimmer with a strange, pellucid light while other parts were plunged in deep velvet blackness. Shutters hung from broken, empty windows and the dilapidated wooden sidewalk was splintered and full of gaping holes. The dust lay ankle-deep, muffling the sound of his horse's hoofs and the wagon wheels. As he rode through the burned out district where he had once lived, he fancied he could still detect the acrid smell of smoke and ash. As he left the ghost town behind, the cool night air carried the tangy scent of pine.

He rode on as dawn broke and the day advanced towards noon. The sun beat down and he took a couple of halts to rest and water the horse, but otherwise he didn't stop till he reached Granton. It had formerly been quite a small settlement, like many others, with the usual assemblage of false-fronted frame buildings, until the arrival of Mossman's stage line. Now there was a bustle about it. Buckhorn's loss had been Granton's gain. Maybe he had been wrong to fight Mossman. After all, did it really matter whether Granton or Buckhorn had the business? As marshal of Buckhorn, he had felt it part of his duty to take on Mossman, but it had been like fighting a spectre. Mossman's subtle influence was all pervasive. There were plenty of stories about his dubious business dealings but it was impossible to pin anything on him. Mossman was too powerful. The whole matter had been finally settled when a portion of Buckhorn was destroyed in a raging conflagration. It had taken the fire to finally settle the matter.

Outside the grocery store he dismounted and tied his horse to the hitch rack. He glanced up and down the street. It was unusually quiet but that suited him. As he entered the store, a bell jangled and after a moment the proprietor appeared. He peered at Lowell for a few moments before recognizing him.

'Why, it's you, Lowell,' he said. 'We don't get to see you very often.'

'Hello,' Lowell said. 'Nope, I guess not. I just stopped by to pick up a few things.'

' "Stopped by"? Hell, I'd hardly call it that. Don't you ever think. . . ?'

He didn't continue but instead glanced through the window. Lowell, detecting something in his manner, turned round and looked too. Three men were crossing the street. They stopped for a moment and one of them examined Lowell's buck-board.

'They look like some of Rickard's men,' the storekeeper said.

Lowell was expecting them to come into the store but instead they turned and began to walk away. Lowell exchanged glances with the store man.

'That's odd,' he said.

Suddenly he sprang to the door and, flinging it open, dashed into the street. The men had moved a little way but one of them turned at his appearance.

'You boys lookin' for somebody?' Lowell shouted.

The response was instantaneous as all three men reached for their guns. Lowell had the advantage, however. They were turning and the sun was behind him. Their shots flew high and wide but Lowell's return fire was accurate. Two of them went down and the third began to run. Lowell was about to set off after him when he heard someone yell:

'Look out!'

At the same moment, shots rang out behind him and he felt a searing pain as a bullet tore into his shoulder. He turned to see two men advancing on him, their guns spitting lead. As he threw himself down he heard another shot and one of the men fell to the ground. Out of the corner of his eye he saw a man standing on the boardwalk just in the lee of a shop awning, a smoking gun in his hand.

'Quick, get into the buckboard!' the man shouted.

Lowell's hand squeezed the trigger of his .44 and as the second man crumpled, he got to his feet and, running to the buckboard, threw himself inside. The man had already taken the driver's seat and with a flick of the reins he quickly had the wagon in motion. As it gathered speed and began to rumble down the street, Lowell observed that several more gunmen had appeared. Some of them were running after the buckboard but a shot from his six-gun soon brought them to a halt. The buckboard clattered on, raising a cloud of dust which helped to screen them from further fire. He looked ahead and saw a figure coming from that direction.

'The marshal!' the driver shouted. 'We can do without more complications!'

They were approaching a junction and as he turned the wagon into it, the wheels on the near side left the ground and they almost overturned. The buckboard came down with a bump which shook every bone in Lowell's body. They carried on at breakneck speed, passing the last faded buildings as they left the town behind them. The driver didn't let up but carried on at dizzying speed. Lowell was being jolted and bounced as he tried desperately to hold on to the sides of the buckboard. They kept on going till at last the driver slowed, but he still carried on for a while before finally drawing the horse to a halt. It stood in the traces, sweating and steaming, its mouth and nose lathered. The man leaned over.

'Are you OK?' he said.

'I've been hit but I don't think it's serious.'

The man climbed down from the driver's seat. 'Low-down varmints,' he said. 'I saw what happened. Here, let me take a look.'

With some difficulty, Lowell unbuttoned his shirt and peeled it back. He felt blood running down his back.

'You've taken one just under the shoulder blade,' the man said. 'It's quite bad but I don't think anything's broken. We need to do somethin' to stop the bleedin'.'

So saying, he ripped off his neckerchief and placed it firmly against the wound, using Lowell's bandana to help keep it in place.

'The bullet wants removin',' he said. When he had finished, he stood up and looked around him.

'We've still a ways to go but I figure we're safe from pursuit.'

'I got to thank you for this,' Lowell said. 'If you hadn't have stepped in, I figure I'd be dead now.'

The other man shrugged. 'I don't like back-shooters. Let's just say I helped even the odds a little.' He looked more closely at Lowell.

'Say,' he said, 'I know it ain't none of my business, but ain't you the feller lives by himself in that old ghost town?'

'Yes, that'd be me.'

'Lowell, ain't it? I've heard your name once or twice around town. Well, I'm Eliot. You might know the name. I'm Jordan Fuller Eliot. I'm related to the Fullers of Nelson County.'

The man's words caught Lowell by surprise and he took a moment or two to collect his thoughts.

'You know Bark Fuller?' he eventually replied.

'He used to run a spread called the Flying Six.'

'He runs one called the Long Rail now. It ain't long since he took it over. It's still a new country to him. I'm a kind of distant cousin. I ride for the Long Rail.'

'You're related to Bark Fuller!' Lowell exclaimed. 'Well, I'll be.'

'Like I say, kind of distant.'

'Me and Bark rode together one time. How is the old coot?'

'He's kinda findin' his feet but he's fine. He'll make a go of the Long Rail.' He stopped and looked around. Lowell had the feeling he was holding something back. Was the Long Rail in some kind of difficulty?

'I guess we'd better carry on,' he continued. 'Question is, where to?'

'It's a fair way to Buckhorn. I can take over now.' Lowell made to get up but sank back in pain.

'Whoa!' Eliot said. 'Try and take it easy. You're in no state to be doin' anythin'. You need a doc. Besides, you're forgettin' somethin'. I left my horse behind.' He thought for a moment.

'Of course,' he said. 'The answer is starin' us in the face. You can come with me back to the Long Rail.'

'Bark Fuller's spread?'

'Sure. I expect he'd be glad to see you again. It ain't too far. I'm surprised you and Bark ain't run into each other. You'd have time to recover and if those gunslicks are still gunnin' for you, they'd never think of lookin' for you there.'

Lowell felt a certain reluctance to involve Eliot any further but a moment's reflection suggested that it might be the best answer. He didn't have a lot of choice.

'OK,' he said. The pain in his back was steadily increasing and he was beginning to feel faint. His head felt misty. With a grim determination he managed to pull himself together.

'Take a look under the seat', he said. 'You'll find a bottle of whiskey.'

Eliot chuckled. 'You figure it'll still be in one piece?' He rummaged about for a moment before coming up with it intact. He handed it to Lowell who took a few swigs and passed it back. Eliot did the same.

'Keep takin' a pull,' he said. 'Give me a shout if things get bad. The buckboard ain't too comfortable.'

With a last glance about him, he climbed into the driver's seat and they continued on their way.

Lowell lay back, trying to concentrate his thoughts. It was pretty clear that he had been the target of a concerted attack on his life. It was only by dint of luck and the intervention of the stranger that he had survived. Who would want him dead? He couldn't make any sense of it. Presently he began to nod off to the rhythm of the wagon wheels. He dozed fitfully till a jolt of the buckboard brought him fully awake again. Some time had obviously elapsed because night had fallen.

'Not much further,' he heard Eliot shout. 'This is Long Rail range.'

Lowell was feeling a bit better and made an effort to observe his surroundings. It was clearly a decent spread. Cattle were standing in bunches and even in the dark they looked sleek.

'Soon be time for the roundup,' Eliot remarked.

During the course of the ride he had kept talking to Lowell, even though he knew he was probably asleep.

'I tell you what,' he said. 'Once you've gotten over that wound, I reckon you could have a job if you wanted it. A man of your experience would come in mighty useful. You've worked for Bark before.'

'That was a long time ago,' Lowell replied, 'before he ever acquired the Long Rail. Anyway, I expect Bark will have all the men he needs.'

The buckboard lumbered on. Even though it

was night, swarms of flies hung about them and were attracted by Lowell's wound. Eliot had suggested changing the makeshift bandage but he had waved him away. He had succeeded in at least staunching the flow of blood and Lowell didn't want to risk opening it up again.

A mist seemed to be gathering at the edges of his vision when he heard Eliot say, 'Look, we've arrived. There's the ranch-house.'

He raised his sagging head. A little way ahead stood an impressive two storey building backed by some outbuildings and a couple of corrals. A shade tree stood in one corner of the yard. As the buckboard drove into the yard, the door of the building opened and a couple of figures appeared.

'Jordan, is that you?' the first man remarked.

'Hello, Bark,' Eliot said. 'I've got someone with me. You might remember him. It's an old friend of yours: Burt Lowell.'

'Burt Lowell! Well, I'll be. . . .'

'He's been shot. He needs assistance. Help me get him down.'

Bark and the man with him sprang to the buckboard and helped lift him out.

'We'll take him straight inside and put him in the spare room,' Bark said to Eliot.

The three men made light work of carrying

Lowell through the main lounge of the ranch-house and into a room behind. As gently as they could they lifted him on to a bunk. Lowell looked up, seeking his old friend, but the mist before his eyes had grown into a cloud which enveloped him. He couldn't tell before he finally lapsed into unconsciousness whether the face which suddenly hovered before him was the face of a woman or an angel or whether the whole thing was an illusion.

The face which presented itself when he awoke was certainly not the countenance of either a woman or an angel. It wore a close brown beard flecked with grey and had a distinctive long, red-dened and somewhat bulbous nose. Above the right temple was a deep scar. It seemed somehow familiar. Struggling with a memory, Lowell attempted to sit up but didn't get very far as a sharp pain in his shoulder region made him sink back again.

'Take it easy,' the man said. 'You don't want to go rushin' things and risk a set-back when you've got this far.'

Lowell turned his head to take in something of his surroundings. A window was open and a refreshing breeze blew into the room. On one wall hung a large framed print of a hunting scene. Something about it held his attention.

'You like the picture?' the man said. 'It's called *Woodcock Shooting*.'

'It looks a mite different to buffalo huntin',' Lowell responded.

Fuller grinned. 'It's nice, isn't it? Oh, nothin' to do with me. I ain't picked up any more culture since the last time we met. Nope. If this old place has anythin' to recommend it, it's down to Lorna.'

'Lorna?' Lowell said.

'My niece.'

Again, Lowell struggled to remember. 'So I wasn't imaginin' it. I thought I saw a woman's face.'

'Yup. That would be Lorna. I can tell you; you've got a lot to thank her for. Since the doc dug that bullet out of you, she's spent a lot of time helpin' to pull you through. And Eliot too.' Suddenly the man's face broke into a grin.

'Hell,' he said, 'I sure didn't expect to see you again. At least not like this. Don't you recognize me? I'm your old partner, Bark Fuller. I can't have changed that much.' He fingered the scar on his brow. 'Don't think I had this last time. Horse kick. Almost did for me.'

His words had the effect of loosening something in Lowell. Suddenly he no longer felt strange or confused. The reality of his situation flooded in and it was with a huge sense of relief

18

that he recognized his old friend.

'Bark, it's sure good to see you again.'

'It's been a long time. But it seems like you ain't been livin' too far away. How come we ain't bumped into each other before now?'

His question caught Lowell unprepared. 'I guess you could say I've been lyin' kinda low,' he said.

'Well, you don't need to do that anymore. Eliot was sayin' you might need a job. Once you're fully recovered, of course. You don't need to look any further. There's a job for you right here on the Long Rail.'

'That's a nice offer, but I ain't so sure. I wouldn't want to take advantage.'

Fuller laughed. 'For a moment there I thought it was the fever talkin'. You won't be takin' advantage, man. There's a whole heap of work to be done and I'm short of hands.'

'Why is that?' Lowell said. 'I'd have thought there'd be no bother findin' men. There are plenty of cowhands lookin' for work at this time of year.'

Fuller's jovial mood seemed to vanish. A worried look came over his features.

'Normally that would be the case,' he said. 'But right now things just ain't normal.'

Lowell was suddenly interested. 'Go on,' he prompted.

By way of answer Fuller rose to his feet. 'Never mind all that just now,' he said. 'I didn't come in here to start gettin' you all worked up. Seems like you're recoverin', but you need to take it easy.'

He glanced up, looking through the door. 'Besides, I ain't the only one waitin' to see you. Here comes Lorna right now.'

Lowell turned his head at the sound of footsteps and the swish of a skirt. In a moment a woman appeared in the doorway carrying a tray on which stood some bread and a bowl of broth. Fuller grinned.

'I'll leave you to it,' he said.

Lowell made an effort to sit up and this time he was successful. 'Talk to you again,' he said. 'By the way, how long have I been here?'

'Two days,' the girl replied.

'Nearer three,' Fuller said. 'See you later.' He went out of the room and the girl sat on the chair he had vacated.

'Can you manage?' she said, offering him the food.

Lowell nodded. He took a sip of the broth. It tasted good and he said so. While he was eating, he observed his companion and liked what he saw. He reckoned she must be in her early twenties. She had thick auburn hair done in ringlets and her

20

plain gingham dress only emphasized the lines of her figure.

'How are you feeling?' she asked.

'A lot better than I did,' he replied. He didn't mention how his head was pounding or the ache in his shoulder.

'I suppose I had better introduce myself,' she said. 'I'm Lorna. I'm Mr Fuller's niece.'

'I'm very glad to meet you. I'm Burt Lowell. I understand I owe you thanks for attending to me.'

He suddenly felt awkward, wondering if he had said the right thing, but she quickly put him at his ease.

'There's no need for thanks,' she said. 'I'm afraid I'm not much of a nurse. I probably did all the wrong things.'

He wondered just how much he was in her debt. His wound had obviously been recently bandaged. Instead of pursuing the topic, however, he pointed to the print instead.

'Your uncle tells me the picture is yours,' he said.

She looked up. 'You like it?' she asked.

'Yes, I do.'

'It's by Currier and Ives,' she replied. 'The original painting was done by a lady named Fanny Palmer. I knew her a little, back in New York. She's an old lady now. If you look hard, you might just be

21

able to see her signature.'

Lowell made to get up but seeing the grimace on his face, Lorna put her hand gently on his arm.

'Maybe not just now,' she said.

He sank back again and resumed his broth. When he had finished she got to her feet and picked up the tray.

'Try and get some rest,' she said.

When she had gone, closing the door softly behind her, Lowell lay for some time with his head propped against the pillow, looking at the sky through the open window. The broth seemed to have done him some good. The pounding in his head began to fade as he drifted into slumber.

When he awoke he felt a lot better. The light had faded but the breeze outside seemed to have picked up. Gingerly, he raised himself and swung first one leg over the edge of the bunk and then the other. He sat for a while before, placing his hands on the bed-frame, he hauled himself upright. Behind the bed was a chair he had not previously noticed and on it his clothes were piled. He had some problems pulling them on but he finally succeeded. His gun belt was slung across the back of the chair and he strapped it round his waist. He had no clear idea about what he intended to do, and was just considering the matter when he heard voices coming through the open window.

'It seems like he's been livin' in that old ghost town. Why would a man want to spend any time there?'

'I don't know. He kept mumblin' somethin' when the fever was on him – sounded like a name but I couldn't make it out.'

'If folks in town knew he was livin' like a wounded coyote, they should have done somethin' about it.'

'What could anyone do, if that was his choice? One thing I picked up: he used to be the Buckhorn marshal one time. I guess it was still a functioning community then.'

Lowell recognized the voices of Eliot and Fuller. There was a moment's pause before Fuller spoke again.

'Well, whatever this is all about, I figure we'd better be prepared. Those gunslicks could come lookin' for him again. To tell you the truth, I'm a bit surprised they ain't got here already. You and Lowell must have left some sign.'

'I guess none of them is any good at trackin'. But what happened to Lowell ain't that unusual. Seems like it's gettin' to be unsafe just goin' about town. Matters have been gettin' worse and worse in Granton. The murder of Brownlow was just the culmination of a lot of bad things.'

'I knew Brownlow. He was a good man.'

'Yeah. He did a lot to help the town. I don't hold out a lot of hope that whoever did it will be caught either, not since Fowler took over as marshal. It ain't no use lookin' for justice there. If there's any justice to be had, it'll be tough justice. Folks'll have to look out for themselves.'

There was a pause before the voice resumed.

'There's somethin' else I've been thinkin' about. Some of the cattle have been stolen and we both reckon maybe Rickard's behind it. I know it seems like a different matter entirely, but you don't suppose there could be some connection?'

'What? With what happened to Lowell?'

'Yeah. Maybe all this trouble comin' at once is more than a coincidence.'

'You could be right. On the other hand, maybe we're wrong about Rickard. Maybe we've been doin' him an injustice. All the same, I just don't take to the idea of those cattalo critters he's got back there at the Half-Box M.'

'Cattaloes?'

'Crossbreeds,' Fuller said. 'Buffalo-cattle off-spring. You ain't heard of 'em? I think it's a spin-off from that buffalo hide business he runs. I wouldn't mind any of it so much except for Lorna. I've tried to shield her, but I think she's cottoned that matters ain't quite what they should be. I wouldn't want her to get caught up in anything.'

Lowell heard the sound of boots and the talk dwindled as the two men walked away. For a few moments he stood quietly, thinking over what he had just heard. He wasn't sure what to make of it all. He was caught in a welter of indecision. Through all his confusion the name of Rickard stood clear. It wasn't the first time he had heard it mentioned. The storekeeper had referred to him too. It seemed Rickard was an influential man around Granton. Although his visits to the town were relatively few, he had picked up some of the gossip.

He felt reluctant to embroil other people in his own struggles. First Eliot had come to his rescue, and now his old friend Fuller was involved. There was also Fuller's niece to worry about. He didn't know what she was doing there, but that was irrelevant. Fuller himself had voiced his concerns about her. It seemed to him that the best thing would be make an exit and do it quickly. Suddenly purposeful, he looked out of the window. There was no sign of Fuller or Eliot. The window looked out on the corral. There were some horses in it but he couldn't see his own sorrel or the buckboard either.

Chances were that the building to the right was the stable. In all likelihood, he would find his horse and his saddle in there. Bracing himself against the pain in his shoulder, he climbed awkwardly out of the window.

There was more of a drop than he had allowed for and he landed awkwardly, jarring his shoulder. He remained crouched for a minute or two, gathering his breath, before beginning to creep towards the stable building. He kept looking out for Fuller and Eliot, but he couldn't see them. Just as he approached the stable the door of another building was flung open and two men came out, talking together. Lowell ran the last few yards to the stable, doubled over, and pressed himself against the wall. A light had come on in the building from which the men had emerged and from time to time he heard the sound of voices. He guessed it was the bunkhouse. Inching his way to the stable door, he peered inside.

It was gloomy but he could see a number of horses in their stalls. The smell of horse-flesh and manure was strong. Still keeping low, he moved inside. He was in luck. The place was deserted. He began to look around for his own horse but he couldn't see it. He moved to the rear entrance and, glancing outside, saw a dusty yard with the buckboard standing in it. At the back of the yard was a small corral containing a couple of horses, one of which he recognized as his own sorrel. He turned back inside the stable. A number of saddles hung from pegs and he took one. Rather than try to cross the open yard undetected, he made his way round it by a circuitous route, taking advantage of any cover that offered itself. The corral was sheltered by some trees and bushes at one side and he led the sorrel there to saddle it up. It didn't take very long. It was only as he tightened the girths that he suddenly wondered why he was acting so surreptitiously. After all, Fuller and Eliot were on his side. He assuaged his conscience with the thought that he was doing it for their good. Maybe he had got out of the habit of being with people. In any case, he had made his decision and there was no point in changing his mind. With a last look round to make sure there was no one about, he climbed into leather and turned away from the Long Rail.

He rode hard till he was well clear of the ranch-house before slowing the sorrel and allowing it to go at its own pace. As darkness descended he saw an overgrown dugout and, after a moment's thought, decided to stay there overnight. The place was at a remote stretch of the range and looked as though it hadn't been occupied for some time. It was probably only used in winter as a base to stop the cattle from drifting. When he looked inside, his initial impression was confirmed. The place was very sparsely furnished with a cheap pine table, a couple of straight-backed chairs held together with baling wire and a rusty iron bed frame without a mattress, but it would serve his purposes.

He knew that he wasn't thinking straight. It might even be the lingering effects of the fever he had been through. At least the place offered him a temporary refuge. His absence from the ranch-house would soon be discovered and a pursuit instigated but nobody would think of looking for him here and he intended being on his way again before dawn. In the meantime he needed more time to think.

He made himself as comfortable as possible, making coffee from the supplies he always carried in his saddle-bags, rolling a cigarette and trying to organize his scattered thoughts. His intention remained to seek out the man both Fuller and Eliot had referred to: Rickard. He had a vague sense that he would be riding into a mess of trouble but the knowledge was not sufficient to deter him. He began to consider the name. Had he ever come across it before? Search his memory as he might, he could not recall any incident involving a man named Rickard. Maybe Eliot was barking up the wrong tree entirely when he thought there might be a connection between what had happened to him and whatever trouble seemed to be brewing with regard to the Long Rail. Someone had mentioned a ranch in connection with Rickard but what was it? Either Fuller or Eliot had mentioned a name. He should be able to remember it. He tried going through the names of some of the ranches in the area. That was it: the Half-Box M. Should he make his way there? No, he would head for Granton and see what he could find out in town.

CHAPTER TWO

The township of Granton was like a lot of others, but there was a certain bustle about the place because of its stage-line connection. All along Front Street stacks of buffalo hides towered, and over the entrance to one of the bigger buildings was the name *Ludwig Rickard, Animal Hides, Pelts and Fertilizer.* The owner of the business was sitting on the edge of a windowsill, looking down on the scene below.

His attention was soon drawn to a stocky figure in buckskin that emerged from the Fashion Restaurant and made its way across the street in his direction. When the man disappeared under an awning, he turned back into the room and sat down at a large leather-topped desk. After a few moments the door opened and the face of his secretary appeared.

'Mr Vernon to see you. I told him you were busy, but he seems rather anxious.'

Rickard grimaced and thought for a moment before replying:

'Ok, show him in.'

She turned and made a gesture and the man appeared. She shut the door behind him.

'Well, Vernon, this is an unexpected pleasure,' Rickard said.

The man was hesitant and Rickard didn't do anything to put him at his ease. He advanced slowly towards Rickard's desk.

'Well,' Rickard said, 'can I be of help?'

Vernon seemed to be steeling himself to speak. 'I want my money,' he finally managed to say.

'And you shall have it,' Rickard answered. 'Every last cent of it.'

'You told me that before.'

'I said there might be a temporary delay. That little impediment has now passed. In fact, I was in the very process of arranging for a transfer of cash to your account.'

'I don't know what you're talkin' about,' Vernon replied.

'Of course; my mistake. Here, let me write you a cheque.'

'I don't want no cheque. Just give me my money.'

Rickard smiled. 'Of course, I understand,' he said. 'If you'll excuse me a moment, I'll be right back.'

He crossed the room and went out the door. Vernon remained standing, awkwardly looking around him. The sounds of the street entered through the open window. In a few minutes the door opened and Rickard re-entered. He was carrying a bundle wrapped in brown paper which he handed over to Vernon.

'There you are: the full amount plus a little extra to make up for the delay. You can count it if you like.'

Vernon hesitated a moment and then thrust the bundle into an inside pocket.

'If you're interested,' Rickard continued, 'I could put a little further work your way.'

'More buffalo huntin'?' the man replied.

'I may require your services again in that department,' Rickard replied, 'but not just for the moment. Stocks are pretty high, as you might have seen. No, it's something else I have in mind.'

'What? You mean. . . .'

'Yes. You did a good job dealing with Brownlow. Now there's someone else who, shall we say, needs teaching a lesson.'

'You want me to do the same?'

'I leave that entirely up to you. I don't question your methods.'

Vernon's face crumpled into an ugly grin. 'Leave it to me, Mr Rickard,' he said.

'Rest assured,' Rickard replied, 'you will be paid in full and promptly. As I said, the previous delay was purely due to a minor cash flow problem. Now I've succeeded in finding a market and those hides are waiting to be sent off, that situation isn't likely to arise again.'

Vernon swallowed and then licked his lips. 'Who have you got in mind this time?' he ventured.

'A man named Burt Lowell. You might know of him. Apparently he's a loner and has been spending most of his time in that old ghost town – Buckhorn I think they call it.'

'I know the place. It should be easy enough to deal with him.'

'That's what I thought. Unfortunately, it doesn't always turn out that way.'

Vernon looked puzzled.

'I expect you've heard about the recent shooting in town. That was Lowell's doing. Those men he shot were from the Half-Box M.' Rickard's expression suddenly turned thunderous.

'Incompetent idiots,' he hissed. 'It wasn't just me they failed. It wasn't just me they were responsible to.' He paused while the flash of anger subsided.

'Anyway,' he continued. 'You've proved your worth. Your reputation precedes you and I know I can trust you to get the job done. I can tell you, there'll be good money in it this time.'

'Is Lowell connected with Brownlow?'

'That is no concern of yours. Brownlow went too far with some of his scurrilous articles aimed both at me and Mr Mossman,' Rickard replied. 'All lies. All lies. Let's just say that this time it's personal.'

He suddenly seemed to lose interest in pursuing the topic any further. He got to his feet as a signal that the interview was over and Vernon took the hint. Rickard accompanied him to the door.

'My secretary will give you any further information you might require regarding Lowell,' he said. 'Just make sure you don't let me down.'

Vernon grinned. 'You know you can rely on me,' he said. 'You won't need to bother about Lowell anymore.'

Rickard opened the door to usher Vernon out. When he had closed it behind him he returned to his desk and poured another drink. He didn't like Vernon. He already knew too much and in his burst of anger he had given more away than he had intended. In particular, he should never have mentioned the name of Mossman. His whole position required him to be discreet. After all, he depended on Mossman. It wouldn't do to antagonize him in any way. Once Vernon had carried out his latest assignment, it might be wise to deal with him too.

The more Lowell thought about his situation, the less he could make of it. He sat in the dugout smoking one cigarette after another, racking his brains, but he still couldn't come up with a reason why anybody would want him dead. For a long time he had been more or less out of the flow of affairs altogether. So it must have something to do with his past. Yet whoever was behind it certainly knew where to find him. He was able to employ people to do his dirty work. Was it a gang operating in the area? He suddenly had a glimmer of inspiration. Maybe they were ranch-hands. That would tie in with what he had overheard Eliot and Fuller say. He pondered again whether or not he should make for the Half-Box M but decided to stay with his initial plan.

Time passed and his thoughts came to a stop as his shoulder began to hurt. Getting to his feet, he went through the pockets of his jacket, bringing out a piece of broken mirror. Holding it in position, he examined the wound as best he could in the flickering candlelight. He was pleased with the results. It looked clean and on the mend. That being the case, he could cope with a little discomfort. He turned away and made his way outside where he stood for a while, breathing in the clean night air. The sky was filled with stars which cast a pale glow over the range. He felt refreshed. He was about to turn away when he thought he saw a flicker of movement in the distance. He stared intently. It was a rider. He slipped back inside the dugout and emerged with his rifle. For the moment he had lost sight of him and might have been tempted to believe he had been mistaken when his ears picked up the horse's hoof-beats. It was moving very slowly. Lowell was puzzled. Why was it going at that pace? The rider came back in sight, and as he got closer something about him seemed familiar and it came as no real surprise when a voice rang out:

'Lowell! Are you in there? It's me, Eliot!'

Lowell lowered his rifle. 'I'm here,' he said. 'but what the hell are you doin'?'

Eliot came up and dismounted. 'You seem to be makin' a habit of hidin' out in places like this,' he said.

'How did you find me?'

'Isn't it obvious? I simply followed your sign.'

A sudden thought struck Lowell and he peered

out into the night. 'Is anybody else with you?' he asked. Eliot shook his head.

'Nope. I had a notion you might not appreciate it if we showed up in numbers.'

'Come on in. I'll make some coffee.'

Eliot seemed hesitant.

'Fuller's worried about you,' he said. 'So is Lorna. Why did you take off without tellin' anybody?'

'I'm sorry. I could have handled things better. I guess I wasn't thinkin' straight.'

'Then come on back with me.'

Lowell shook his head.

'Nope. I've been doin' some thinkin' and there's somethin' I have to do.'

'Yeah. What's that?'

'I heard you and Fuller talkin' about Rickard. I figure he might be worth payin' a visit. I've decided I'm goin' back to Granton and see Rickard.'

'You're not really serious? Have you forgot what happened back there? You'll be walkin' straight into a trap. You only need to show your face and you'll be a sittin' target.'

'I've thought about that.'

'Wouldn't it be more sensible to come back to the Long Rail with me?'

'Maybe. But I don't want to do that. I'd be

puttin' the place at risk.'

'We could round up a few men and then ride to Granton in force.'

'That wouldn't work. It's gonna take somethin' a bit more subtle to worm the truth out of Rickard. Besides, if the Long Rail's under any sort of threat, it would be foolish to take anybody away. That would just make it all the more vulnerable.'

'I can see you ain't gonna change your mind,' Eliot said. 'In that case, any objections to me comin' along as back-up?'

'You've done enough for me already. Nope, the same thing applies. If there's any trouble here, you're gonna be needed. You can give my apologies to Fuller, though. I guess the way I left wasn't exactly right. And you can tell me what else you know about Rickard.'

Eliot looked closely at him. 'You could still do with givin' yourself some time for that wound to get better. At least stay on here for a day or two till you're fully fit.'

Lowell nodded. 'I feel fine, but I guess that kinda makes sense.'

All this while Eliot had remained in the saddle but he finally dismounted. 'If it's OK with you,' he said, 'I could sure use a cup of coffee.'

*

38

Lowell took up Eliot's suggestion and waited a few days till he felt he was fully recovered before starting for Granton. He was pleased to get away. Before he left, Eliot had made further appeals for Lowell to accompany him back to the Long Rail. His arguments made a lot of sense, probably a lot more that Lowell's plans. However, after a lot of troubled thinking, he had decided on a course of action and now he intended seeing it through. It had been useful talking things over with Eliot, however. He had been able to give Lowell more information on Rickard and the state of affairs in Granton. One thing he had intended doing was to pay a call on the marshal. Now he knew that might not be a wise thing to do. From what Eliot had told him, it seemed the marshal owed his position to Rickard. Basically, he was on Rickard's payroll.

He rode at a steady pace until around noon he began to observe buzzards wheeling and circling in the sky. The sorrel pricked up its ears and was obviously agitated. As he continued the smell of death assailed his nostrils. He had seen small groups of buffalo, mainly males, and somehow he knew what to expect.

'Buffalo hunters,' he said to his horse. 'I hate 'em.'

As he topped a rise the scene of slaughter lay

spread out below. All across the prairie the corpses of buffalo rotted in the heat. Dense swarms of flies hung in the air as buzzards and prairie wolves fought over the remains. He knew that the practice had arisen of shooting them from the railroad cars, but it seemed the slaughter here was even more wanton. Whoever was responsible must have come across the herd at a buffalo wash and killed them for the fun of it. They hadn't even bothered to skin them, but just left them where they had dropped. Circling in order to avoid the heaped up corpses, he rode on towards Granton.

Vernon closed the door of the Fashion Restaurant behind him and stepped out on to the boardwalk. He had just eaten and he was feeling a little heavy. He walked slowly till he reached the saloon where he paused before entering. He leaned against the balustrade, looking towards the stacks of hides outside Rickard's imposing emporium, waiting to be shipped out. The sun was high and their smell was strong. The air shimmered in the heat and through it he perceived a horseman approaching him. Something about the figure held his attention but it was only when the man was almost upon him that he realized with a start that it was Burt Lowell, the very man he had been commissioned to kill. He couldn't be absolutely certain; he had only seen Lowell around town a couple of times, but he was quite an arresting figure. His immediate thought was how unfortunate it was that he wasn't prepared, but then, how could he have known? The best thing to do would be to follow his movements and wait for the chance which was sure to come. Then he had another idea. Quickly, he began to make his way towards the marshal's office.

Lowell rode directly to the building across which the lettering *Ludwig Rickard, Animal Hides and Fertiliser* was written in bold lettering, where he dismounted and tied his horse to the hitch rack. Inside, an arrow directed him up a flight of stairs. A young lady sat at a desk beyond which was a heavy door with frosted glass. She looked up at his approach.

'Can I help you?' she asked. Her voice and manner were like a shard of ice.

'I've come to see Rickard,' he replied.

'Have you an appointment?'

'Nope. Do I need one?'

'I'm sorry. No one can see Mr Rickard without having an appointment.'

Lowell hesitated for a moment and then stepped past the desk and, advancing to the door beyond, flung it open. The room was empty. The woman rose from her chair.

'I was about to tell you that Mr Rickard is not available.'

'Where is he?'

'I don't think that's any of your business.'

Lowell felt outmanoeuvred. Turning away, he began to make for the stairs. Just before he commenced the descent he turned to the woman.

'Apologies ma'am, if my behaviour was a little abrupt. It's just that . . . maybe I could make an appointment.'

'I'm afraid Mr Rickard's diary is full for the foreseeable future.'

He put his foot on the stair.

'Who should I say was looking for him,' she said.

'Lowell, Burt Lowell. You can tell him I'll be back.'

'I can assure you there wouldn't be any point.'

Lowell clattered down the stairs. Was Rickard in town? He would stay around for a while and hopefully run into him. If not, there was the Half-Box M.

When he was outside he took time to look up and down the street, his face puckering as he sniffed the air. The smell made him want a drink. Just a little way down the street stood the Starlight Saloon and he began to make his way towards it.

His eye was attracted to a man wearing buckskins who leaned against a stanchion, deep in conversation with another man. He did not take in much else; it was the man's odd choice of garments that he noticed. They seemed entirely unsuited to the heat. He brushed past them both and went through the batwing doors. Evening was approaching and the place was beginning to fill up. He made his way to the bar and placed his foot on the rail.

'What'll it be?' the bartender asked.

'Make it a beer.'

He felt dusty and dry. Even inside the saloon, the smell of buffalo hides hung in the air, combined with stale tobacco, sweat and sawdust. As the barman placed his drink on the counter in front of him, he saw through the mirror behind the bar a man enter wearing a star. Just behind him was the man in buckskins. The marshal was evidently the man with whom he had been in conversation. The marshal paused for a moment, looking around, and Lowell knew instinctively who he was looking for. Already he was piecing things together.

Seeing Lowell standing at the bar, the marshal made his approach. The other man followed close behind.

'That your horse outside?' the marshal said

without any preliminaries.

Lowell had left his horse near Rickard's establishment. In any event, there were several horses outside. 'Nope,' he replied.

The marshal turned to the man in the buckskin jacket and then back to Lowell. 'This gentleman tells me it's your horse.'

'The gentleman is lying. What about it anyway?'

Suddenly Lowell found himself looking down the barrel of the marshal's gun. 'I'm goin' to have to ask you to accompany me to the jailhouse,' he said.

A quiet had descended on the room. People had stopped what they were doing and were looking towards the bar.

'I don't know what this is about,' Lowell said, 'but if you give me a chance to finish this drink, I'll be happy to comply.'

He was playing for time. He already knew what was happening. Eliot had warned him about the marshal. He was being set up. Whoever the man in the buckskin jacket was, he was in with the marshal. And that meant nothing good could come out of allowing himself to be locked in the jailhouse. He had a feeling that he wouldn't come out of it alive. Before making his move, he carefully examined the features of the man in buckskins through the mirror, fixing his image in his memory. Then, with a sudden movement, he flung the glass of beer in the marshal's face. As the marshal staggered back, he took to his heels and fled.

In a matter of seconds he had crashed through the batwings and was hurtling down the street. A shot rang out but it was only a short distance to where he had left his horse. As more bullets began to fly he set it loose and vaulted into the saddle. A bullet thudded into the wall of the building and as he veered away something caught his eye. He looked up and saw the face of Rickard's secretary peering out of the window. Behind her he thought he detected another figure, but he couldn't be sure. In a matter of moments he was on his way, galloping hell for leather down the dusty street. More lead was being thrown, but as he carried on riding, bent low over the horse's neck, the sounds of shooting began to fade. Without looking back, he carried on pell-mell till the town was behind him, when he finally drew the horse to a stop. Standing in the stirrups, he looked all around for any signs of pursuit but there was nothing to be seen. He drew out his field-glasses and put them to his eyes. Far away in the distance he saw a smudge of dust. It grew bigger and to his ears there came a faint, distant rumbling. For a moment he thought there was a posse on his trail but then he realized it was the overland stage on its approach to Granton.

It was quite a new line, the one which had originally been scheduled to link up with Buckhorn before it went to Granton instead. Mossman was behind that decision and it had spelled the end for Buckhorn. The fire which had destroyed part of the town only confirmed its demise. It had been a troublesome place at best. The irony of it was that it was just when he had tamed Buckhorn so that it became a reasonably civilized place to live that people started to desert it. A lot of them had settled in Granton, even Mossman for a while. Mossman was the real winner. The stagecoach business was only the start. Since then he had acquired a railroad line and its recent extension to Shoshone Flats had created a new railhead there. Now that the loading pens were built, many cattlemen would be spared a long drive along the Chisholm Trail. There were fortunes to be made and Mossman was right at the heart of it all. Where was Mossman now? Almost certainly he had made Shoshone Flats the base of his operations. Having destroyed Buckhorn and built up Granton, the latter had become too small for him. Lowell might have been content to live in Granton himself if. . . .

It didn't do to think too much about it.

Replacing the glasses, he sat his horse for some time thinking about his next move. He couldn't come up with any better plan than to carry on riding to the Half-Box M. It might be worth checking on the status of Rickard's cattle.

Bark Fuller and his foreman, an experienced cowman by name of Hoyt Conrad, were driving in some cattle from rough country on the north side of the ranch. Across the range, clouds of dust indicated where men working in pairs were doing the same, occasionally firing their six-guns to smoke out some of the more recalcitrant cattle from the brush. They were working in a circle, driving towards the designated holding spot, and as the circle got tighter the bunches of cattle grew larger and the dust thicker.

The air was filled with noise: the bawling and bellowing of cattle, the crackling of horns, the pounding of hoofs, the shrill yells and yips of the cowboys. Through the racket Fuller heard the sound of an approaching horse and Conrad rode up close.

'Looks like we got company,' Conrad said.

Fuller looked up to see a rider approaching. Through the haze of dust he didn't recognize his niece till she was almost upon him.

'Lorna,' he said, as she came up alongside. 'What are you doin' out here? This ain't no place for you.'

'I thought I'd better come and tell you. Some men have come. They've got a lawyer with them. I don't understand what it's all about, but I think they want you to sign something.'

'Sign something? Who are they?'

'I don't know. Mr Eliot is with them.'

'Eliot?'

'Yes. He came back not long ago.'

'Was Lowell with him?'

'No. He said he'd found Lowell but he couldn't persuade him to come back. Mr Lowell sends his apologies, but apparently he's gone on to Granton.'

'What in tarnation is he doin' that for?' Fuller expostulated. 'Sorry, Lorna, but he seems to be goin' out of his way to find trouble. He always was a cussed stubborn critter.'

'Do you think he's putting himself in danger?'

'Now don't go worryin' your head over things. Lowell knows how to handle himself.' Fuller turned to Conrad.

'Can you take care of things here for a while?'

'Sure thing, Mr Fuller.'

'It shouldn't take long.' Turning his horse, he

rode off alongside his niece.

As they approached the ranch-house, he saw four horses tied to the hitch-rack, and when they had dismounted he took the opportunity to check their brands, although he was pretty sure in advance what they were. Half-Box M. Taking Lorna by the arm, he stepped up on the veranda and opened the door. Two men were sitting on a chaise-longue and the other two were at the table, one of whom, by the cut of his frock-coat, was obviously the lawyer. Eliot was standing nearby.

'Do you mind going to your room?' Fuller said. 'This is business, but it won't take long.'

'Yes, of course.'

When Lorna had left, Fuller turned to Eliot, ignoring the others.

'Thanks for looking after these gentlemen,' he said.

'No problem. Do you want me to leave too?'

'No, stick around. This could be interestin'.'

The lawyer glanced from Fuller to Eliot and back again.

'I don't want to beat about the bush,' he said. 'My name is Dinsdale. I am an attorney-at-law and I act for Mr Rickard who, among other things, is the owner of the ranch known as the Half-Box M.'

'I know who Rickard is,' Fuller snapped.

49

'Mr Rickard has commissioned me to tell you that, after having made due enquiries, he intends to pursue his claim to the section of the Long Rail ranch known as the east range. I think I may say that his claim is sound and he has every reason to assume that a court will find in his favour. However, in order to avoid unnecessary bother and delay, he is willing to make you an offer for the land.'

'He can go to hell,' Fuller said.

Ignoring the comment, the lawyer produced a slip of paper from his pocket and handed it to Fuller. Fuller took one glance and then laughed out loud.

'This is a mockery,' he said, tearing the paper in two.

'Do I take it that you are refusing the offer?' Dinsdale said.

'Yeah, you're damn right I am. And you can tell Rickard that if he or any of his boys set foot on my property again, I'll see that they get dragged off behind a team of horses.'

At his words one of the men on the chaise-longue sat up and his hand dropped towards his gun-belt.

'I wouldn't do anything foolish,' Fuller said. He turned to the lawyer. 'I think you all had better leave right now.'

Dinsdale got to his feet. 'Is that your final word?' he said.

'Get goin'!' Fuller replied.

The lawyer led the way to the door. As he was going through it, one of the men accompanying him turned to Fuller with an ugly leer across his face.

'Don't worry,' he said. 'We'll be back.'

'That girl of yours sure looks good,' another one said. 'I figure she needs a man.'

Fuller took a step forward but managed to restrain himself as both men burst into ugly laughter, spitting on the veranda as they descended the steps.

'Nice company you keep!' Fuller called to the lawyer as they all mounted up and rode out of the yard. Fuller watched them go before returning inside.

'I know it ain't no business of mine, but what was all that about?' Eliot asked.

'I told you things weren't good around here. Well, it looks like they just got a whole lot worse. I figured Rickard was out to get his hands on the Long Rail. So far his tactics have been designed to wear me down. Now it looks like he's comin' out into the open. I hate to say it, but I think we're gonna have a range war on our hands, because I certainly don't intend givin' way to him or his gunnies.'

'I take it that he hasn't got a claim to any of the property?'

'Of course he hasn't. This has come up before though. The real reason he wants the east range is that the river runs through it. If he gets his hands on the water rights, it won't be just the Long Rail that suffers.'

Just at that moment the door to Lorna's room opened and she came out again. She looked at the troubled faces of Fuller and Eliot.

'Is everything all right?' she said. 'I must say I didn't much like the look of those men.'

Fuller made an effort to smile. 'Everythin's fine,' he said. 'Like I said before, you've no need to worry your head about anything. Now Mr Eliot and me have to get back to roundin' up the cattle. Will you be OK till we're finished?'

'Yes, of course. I have plenty of things to do.'

'If you decide to go for a ride, take one of the men along with you,' Fuller said. He exchanged glances with Eliot. 'I wouldn't like you to run the risk of an accident. Ridin' the range ain't quite like takin' a trot in the park.'

'I won't be ridin' any more today,' she assured

him. 'You get back to work and I'll make somethin' nice to eat for later.'

Fuller grinned. 'It's a deal,' he said.

CHAPTER THREE

It was late in the afternoon when Lowell left Granton and darkness descended as he rode towards the Half-Box M. It suited his purposes. He didn't know exactly what he intended doing, but he was well aware of the fact that was running a big risk. While as yet he had no proof that it was men from the Half-Box M who had sought to kill him, a lot of circumstantial evidence was building up and pointing to the possibility. He still couldn't think of a reason why they would do it, but that was a different matter. Perhaps he would pick up some clues when he reached the Half-Box M. Then he remembered Fuller's words about cattle disappearing. If Rickard was involved, he might be able to find proof.

In fact, it took less time and effort than he had

reckoned. By his calculations, midnight had not been long gone when the presence of cattle alerted him to the fact that he must be on Half-Box range. Looming out of the darkness, the animals stood singly or in groups of two or three. Riding close to where a couple of cows stood, he dropped from the saddle and made his approach. Being careful to do nothing that might spook them, he struck a match and examined the brand. Both of them carried a Long Rail brand. So Fuller was right. The cattle rustling was confirmed and the stolen beasts were ending up at the Half-Box M.

He got back into the saddle but as he rode he took the time to examine more of the cattle. He was curious about what Fuller had said about cattalo cross-breeds and kept an eye open for them. However, he didn't see anything out of the ordinary. Apparently he had struck lucky the first time. Apart from one, the others all bore the Half-Box brand. It would be easy, however, to change a Long Rail brand into a Half-Box M. Fuller was too trusting. He should have chosen a more elaborate identification that would defy any efforts at re-branding. He took a closer look at the Half-Box brand. It was hard to see in the dark, but was the Half-Box symbol above the R a little elongated? Either way, he had seen enough to convince him that Fuller was correct and Rickard was implicated in cattle-rustling. Rickard was a powerful man. What else might he be mixed up in? He didn't seem to be making a lot of effort to conceal his activities either, but if Eliot was right and Rickard had the law in his pocket, it was hardly surprising. The events of that day seemed to prove it.

It seemed a long time since he had set out the previous morning, but in spite of everything that had happened he was feeling remarkably fresh. He was concerned for his horse, however, and decided that it was time to make camp, at least for a few hours. He peered through the blackness, searching for a suitable location. A little way ahead of him a line of trees suggested the presence of water and he rode down to the banks of a stream. It was a good spot. Before long he had tended to the sorrel, built a fire, and boiled water for coffee. He wasn't concerned about anybody seeing the flames; even if somebody was about, he was in a hollow and the trees screened him. He got out the makings and built a smoke.

He felt quite comfortable but strangely lonely. He couldn't understand it. Since Etta had died, he had got used to being by himself. Even before that he had been something of a loner, content to spend nights under the stars with only his horse for company. Being with Etta had brought about changes, but hadn't fundamentally altered him. So why did he feel differently? As his reflections wandered, suddenly he found that he was thinking of Lorna Fuller. He felt guilty but he didn't know why.

Finishing the last of his coffee, he threw the dregs into the fire and got to his feet. He wandered over to his horse and spent a few minutes stroking its face and mane. He walked to the top of the slope leading down to the water and looked out across the range. A yellow moon hung low towards the western horizon. Returning to the stream bank, he felt an urge to enter the water. He took off his boots and shirt and waded into the stream. The water was cold and invigorating. He lay on his back and looked up into the star-filled sky, occasionally moving his arms and legs to resist the slow-moving current. The fire, reduced to a glow, occasionally spluttered. After a time, he rose in the water and splashed his way to the river-bank. Making his way over to the fire, he stamped it out and afterwards took some time to remove any traces that he had been there. His mind felt clear. He had found what he had come looking for. A time might come when he would need to pay a call on the Half-Box M but it wasn't now.

His first thought was to head back to Granton.

He recalled what had happened and thought about the man in the buckskin jacket. He was tempted to go back and see if he could find him, but then he reflected that he could wait. He hadn't been the only one involved; there was the marshal too. He had unfinished business with both of them but after all, no harm had been done. What did that leave? He was still feeling bad about the way he had made his exit from the Long Rail. After some thought, he came to the conclusion that the best thing to do would be to go back there and let Fuller know what he had discovered. The fact remained that it was round-up time and Fuller would need all the help he could get. It was easy to forget the basic things that went on whatever else happened. In all his thinking, he didn't consciously acknowledge the attraction of Lorna Fuller. He saddled up his horse and, as the first intimations of dawn began to hint at the arrival of another day, rode up out of the stream-bed, setting his course for the Long Rail.

Rickard was in a very bad mood. He had just received a message at the telegraph office from no less a person than Mossman himself, asking some awkward questions about his conduct of business in Granton, and more specifically about whether he had dealt with Lowell. As regards the first, he was beginning to wonder himself whether he had perhaps done the wrong thing in trying to go beyond Mossman's instructions. Being put in charge of the Half-Box M in particular had given him plenty of scope for some personal aggrandisement. Mossman would probably not have disapproved but he was wily enough to know when he was being cheated of the profits. As for Lowell, that little matter was proving to be particularly irritating. After all, whatever grudge Mossman held against Lowell, it was not his affair. He barely knew who Lowell was. As far as he was concerned he was a nonentity who did not merit a fraction of the amount of attention he was having to give him. But Mossman was the boss and he could ill afford to rile him any further. It was a long distance between Granton and Shoshone Flats, but Mossman had a long arm and his influence was pervasive.

As if that wasn't sufficient, his lawyer had already reported back on the unsuccessful outcome of his visit to Fuller at the Long Rail. He wasn't surprised. It had been a long shot. Clearly Fuller needed more persuading. The communication from Mossman only made the issue more urgent. Mossman might not appreciate the Half-Box M getting involved in a dispute about water rights, but if the acquisition of the Long Rail could be effected without any lingering consequences, he would almost certainly approve. He could have no objections to a *fait accompli*. The question was: how to proceed? Maybe it was time for his men to redeem themselves after the ghost town fiasco.

Making his way to the Fashion Restaurant, he stomped inside and ordered a pot of coffee. While he drank it, he sat by the window. Outside, the heaped piles of buffalo hides reminded him that he needed to organize their transportation. He observed the general activity, keeping his eyes open for any sight of Vernon. Assuming he had made his way to Buckhorn, it couldn't be long till he got back. He realized he was making an assumption. The cack-handed efforts of his men had only served to drive Lowell away. However, Lowell had been living there for a long time. It was fair to assume that at some point he would return.

He got to thinking about Lowell. What was it that Mossman had against him? What could possibly cause him to want Lowell's removal so much? Whatever it was, it seemed to have come out of the blue. Why had it become so urgent? Suddenly he had a flash of inspiration. Mossman had acquired the stage line and had just concluded an even bigger coup with the establishment of the railroad

link to Shoshone Flats. He could expect to make a
fortune from the shipment of cattle back east.
Could Lowell know something that might upset his
plans? Something Mossman had just realized
himself? If so. . . .

Suddenly he jumped to his feet and, leaving the
coffee almost untouched, made for the door. A
new thought had struck him. If Lowell knew something to Mossman's detriment, it might be in his
own interests to find out just what it was. He might
have made a big mistake in acquiescing with
Mossman's instructions. It might be more sensible
to keep Lowell alive – at least for the time being.
He needed to find Vernon.

Lowell had been somewhat nervous about returning to the Long Rail, but he needn't have worried.
There was no doubting the warmth of Fuller's
welcome. Lowell did not go into any details about
his brief time in Granton, concentrating instead on
informing Fuller about the rustled cattle he had
found on Rickard's range. Fuller in turn told
Lowell about the visit from the lawyer.

'I think we're in for trouble,' he said. 'I reckon
Rickard's gonna be turnin' up the heat.' Lowell
had to agree. 'I want to get those beefs on the trail
as quick as possible now,' Fuller continued. 'We've

rounded up most of the cattle, but there are still a lot of 'em hidin' out in the draws. Do you reckon you and Eliot could help bring 'em in?'

It suited Lowell to get back into some kind of routine. He had been kicking his heels for too long and the prospect of some hard work was a boon. The morning after his arrival he and Eliot rode off for the rough country on the fringes of the ranch.

It was a hard area to cover, with brush-filled ravines and thickets of mesquite and prickly pear. They rode into the coulees to roust up the cattle that had established themselves there but bringing them out was only part of the problem and they had to exercise a lot of care to prevent them circling and getting back in again. It was hard work and sweaty, with a constant risk of getting cut and scratched by the sharp thorns. It took most of the day to roust out some score of cattle and start drifting them towards the holding place. A couple of old bulls kept trying to lead the others and head back for the brush but they rode them tight.

The next day was a repeat of the first, but Lowell was relishing the work. He had struck up a rapport with Eliot and they worked well together. When he lay in his bunk at night, Lowell began to be aware of how much he owed the other man. Eliot had backed him up when he faced the gunslicks, risking his own life in the process. He had taken him back to the Long Rail and helped restore him to health. He had come to seek him at the dugout. He wasn't the only person he had to thank either. There was Fuller and Lorna. Since his return he had not seen much of her but then he had not spent any time around the ranch-house. It came as something of a revelation to him to think about what they had all done. He felt the stirrings of an emotion he had not felt for a long time and for some reason recalled the words someone had once used to describe an experience he had had: like he had been down to the river and restored.

Rickard stood at the window of his office watching as a mule train carrying his buffalo hides pulled away. There were six wagons full of them, pulled by teams of mules and accompanied by swarms of flies. He carried on observing till his view was obscured by intervening buildings and then turned, poured himself a drink and sat down on his leather chair. He remained for a considerable time, plunged in thought, when there was a discreet knock at the door which opened to admit his secretary.

'Mr Vernon to see you,' she said. 'I wouldn't have disturbed you but. . . .'

'That's fine, Miss Lockhart. Show him in.'

This was a stroke of luck. He was beginning to think he might not see Vernon and here he was in person. Vernon shuffled into the room and at a gesture from Rickard took a chair on the opposite side of the desk.

'You were supposed to report to me before now,' he said.

'I'm sorry, Mr Rickard. I haven't been feelin' so well.'

'Too much hard liquor. Well, what have you to say for yourself? Have you dealt with Lowell?'

Rickard could tell by Vernon's shame-faced and embarrassed expression that he had not carried out his commission, but in view of recent developments that was all to the good. He was enjoying seeing Vernon squirm.

'I'm sorry,' Vernon repeated, 'but like I say, I haven't been well. I'm gonna take a ride to Buckhorn tonight.'

'My instructions were quite explicit. I don't like being let down.'

'I won't let you down. I've got the matter in hand.'

Rickard grinned. 'As it turns out, Lowell can wait. I got somethin' else for you now.'

'Anythin', anythin' at all, Mr Rickard.'

'The little job I got in mind should suit you down

to the ground. After all, you like to see yourself as
a buffalo hunter.'

'I saw the mule train pull out of town. You
needin' more hides?'

'Yes, but that's not what I got in mind for the
moment. No, this is a lot easier.'

'What is it?'

'A simple assignment. Just take a ride over to the
Long Rail and shoot a few cows.'

'Wouldn't that be trespassin'?'

Rickard gave out a loud laugh. 'Trespassin',' he
said. 'After all you've got on your slate, you're
worried about trespassin'?'

Concerned that he might have made a mistake,
Vernon was quick to rectify it. 'Of course it ain't a
problem. Just leave it to me.'

'One other thing. Make sure you dump a few
corpses in the river.'

Vernon was puzzled but thought it best not to
ask any questions.

'You say you were meanin' to ride out to that old
ghost town tonight. Well, you can pay a visit to the
Long Rail instead. Take a few of your no-good
cronies along with you if you like.' Vernon got to
his feet.

'And remember, I won't be so tolerant of any
mistakes this time,' Rickard added. 'It's an easy

65

assignment. Just make sure you get it done.'

Vernon made for the door, feeling relieved at the outcome. He had been expecting a lot worse. He slithered out and Rickard heard the sound of his steps going down the stairs. What a little weasel, he thought. But he had his uses. If Fuller's resolve not to sell was not finally undermined by this latest ploy, he was ready for an all-out assault. And if Vernon got caught, it was none of his business. No one would believe anything he said and there would be no proof the Half-Box M was involved. In any case, the marshal was in his pocket. If Vernon got himself killed, so much the better.

On the fourth day after his arrival back at the Long Rail, Lowell and Eliot were working towards the east range. As they approached the river which ran through the property, they saw something lying in the water. Spurring their horses, they rode up close. Blocking the flow of water were the rotting corpses of three cows. The river at this point was quite shallow and a quick examination showed that the cows had been shot.

'This has been done deliberately,' Eliot said. 'Someone's tryin' to contaminate the water supply.'

'Yeah, and I think we can guess who it is,' Lowell replied.

They both dismounted and began to look about for sign. It wasn't hard to find.

'How many of 'em, do you reckon?' Eliot said.

'Probably half a dozen riders. They must have come in the night.'

The grass was flattened where the corpses had been dragged and the riverbank had fallen away.

'Let's see what we can do to get them out,' Eliot said.

It required a considerable effort, but with the help of their horses they succeeded in hauling the dead animals out of the river.

'Better get back to Fuller and let him know what's happened,' Lowell remarked.

'There's not much else Fuller can do,' Eliot replied.

'I wasn't thinkin' just about those cows,' Lowell replied. 'The way I figure it, Rickard has just declared war on the Long Rail.'

'If so, he's chosen a good time – when the boys are fully occupied with the roundup and gettin' ready for the trail drive.'

'Those varmints we fought off back at Granton weren't just regular cowhands either. I figure Rickard ain't averse to hirin' a few gunslingers to back him up.'

'After what happened, they're likely to be

wantin' revenge. This is just the sort of opportunity they'll be lookin' for.'

The smell of the decaying cattle was strong in their nostrils as they turned and started to ride back.

When they reached the ranch, Fuller was standing by one of the corrals with his foreman, Conrad, talking to a little man in a black frock-coat.

'Who's that?' Lowell asked.

'His name is Dinsdale. He's a lawyer. Rickard sure don't waste any time.'

They rode up and dismounted. Fuller turned to them.

'Hello,' he said. 'What are you boys doin' back?'

'We thought you'd better know. There's trouble.'

'What sort of trouble? Conrad asked.

In a few words Eliot told them what they had found at the river. When he had finished Fuller turned his fierce gaze on the lawyer.

'That's the sort of man you're workin' for,' he snapped.

'I don't know what you mean. Are you trying to infer that there's some connection between what your man has just told you and Mr Rickard's latest offer?'

Fuller seemed to explode. 'I reckon I've just

about taken all I can from you!' he exclaimed. 'I think you'd better get on your horse and get away from here just as quick as you can. And I give you fair warnin': you'd better not show your face round here ever again.'

The lawyer seemed to hesitate for a moment but as Fuller advanced on him he took to his heels and made quickly for his horse. As he rode away Fuller turned to the others.

'He was tryin' again to get me to sell up,' he said. He was still furious. 'By Jiminy, I should have taken a whip to the little skunk.'

'What do you intend doin' now?' Conrad asked.

Fuller glanced over the corrals where the cattle had been left without food or water for a day to help tame them down. He regarded them with a practised eye, before pulling some papers out of his pocket.

'I've been lookin' through these bills of sale,' he said. 'Everythin' seems in order. We've added some cows from a couple of the smaller ranches and the brand, number and earmarks of each are all set out. I figure we're just about ready.' He turned to Conrad, who nodded in confirmation.

'Lowell figures we might get a visit from Rickard and his boys,' Eliot said.

'Especially now that you've turned down his

latest offer,' Lowell added.

'Yeah, I figure the same. We'll get right on with the trail drive, but we'll make sure we're ready for anythin' Rickard might do too.'

'It could get rough. Rickard has more men on his side, and that's not countin' the gunnies he seems to have.'

Fuller's expression was grim. 'Just let him come,' he said.

Conrad looked from Eliot to Lowell. He knew the importance of the trail drive. He had worked for Fuller long enough to know what it meant to him and the other small ranchers. Without the money from this drive, they would be likely to go under; even without any added pressure from Rickard.

'I need to talk to you boys further,' Fuller said. 'Come on over tonight after you've eaten.'

They were about to leave when Lowell heard the swish of a skirt and turned round to see Lorna approaching. He had barely seen her since his arrival and he was taken aback at how fresh and appealing she appeared.

'Has that horrible man gone?' she asked.

'Yes. He decided not to stay around for too long.'

'I've made some coffee. There's plenty to go round.'

'I'm sorry, ma'am,' Conrad replied, 'but I'd best be gettin' on with the roundup.'

As he walked away Eliot and Lowell exchanged glances. Lowell would have liked to take up the offer but he answered for them both.

'It's real nice of you,' he said, 'but we've got things to do as well.'

'You're welcome to stick around for a while,' Fuller commented.

'Thanks, but we'd best get goin',' Eliot replied.

'See you tonight, then.'

Eliot and Lowell mounted up and as they rode away, Lowell glanced back to see Lorna watching them with her hand to her eyes to shelter them from the sun.

'That's quite a lady,' Eliot remarked. 'And I tell you something. Fuller tries to wrap her up in cotton wool, but she's a lot tougher than he thinks.'

'What is she doin' at the Long Rail?' Lowell asked.

'I don't know the full story. Her mother was Fuller's sister. Seems like both her parents died and Fuller took her in.'

'So she's been livin' at the Long Rail for a while?'

'Sure. Must be five years or more. She's settled in real good. From what I gather, she really loves it out here. I don't reckon she'd ever want to go back east again.' Eliot gave Lowell a quizzical glance. 'I don't profess to understand these things, but she seems to like you,' he said.

Lowell was hoping he might see Lorna again that evening, but he was disappointed. He, Eliot and Conrad had already eaten at the bunkhouse, and when they arrived Fuller led them to the veranda where a bottle of whiskey and four glasses stood on a low table. They took their seats around the table and he poured.

'Well gentlemen,' he said. 'After what's happened round here recently, I thought it was time we reviewed the situation.'

'There ain't much to review,' Conrad said. 'Rickard has been rilin' us for a long time. We suspected it was him doin' the rustlin' and now Lowell here has confirmed it.'

'He ain't made any secret of the fact he wants to take over the Long Rail,' Fuller said.

'Just like he's taken over half of Granton and put his own man in office.'

'It's thanks to him that the buffalo have about disappeared from these parts. I ain't averse to shootin' the critters, but slaughterin' them wholesale like that just ain't right.'

'If he was successful in gettin' hold of the Long

Rail, there'd be nothin' to stop him takin' over the whole cattle trade.'

'He ain't gonna get his hands on the Long Rail,' Fuller snapped.

'If Rickard is really intendin' to attack the Long Rail, when is he likely to do it?' Conrad asked.

'And what do we do about it?' Eliot added.

Fuller thought for a moment.

'The way I see it,' he said, 'is that Rickard will wait till we have those cattle on the hoof. It would be a lot easier than attackin' the ranch. Besides, if it's the Long Rail he's after, he won't want to damage the property. If he stops those cattle gettin' to the markets, he'll have bankrupted the Long Rail. And maybe not just the Long Rail but some of the other ranches as well.'

'I agree,' Conrad said. 'That's the way I've been lookin' at it too.'

'We ain't got enough men to try and safeguard the ranch and do the drive. Seems to me we concentrate on doin' our best to protect the herd. You never know; we might be wrong and it might never happen.'

'I don't think any of us believe that,' Conrad said. 'But you don't need to have any concerns about the men. They know the situation and just exactly what's expected of 'em.'

'Thanks, Conrad,' Fuller replied. He took a long swig of whiskey. 'There's one thing puzzles me though.'

'Yeah. What's that?' Conrad said.

'I'd like to know to what extent Rickard is operatin' on his own and to what extent he's frontin' for Mossman.'

Lowell was suddenly interested. 'Mossman?' he said.

'Yes. You must have come across the name. He runs the stage line and now he owns a railroad company. They've just extended the line to Shoshone Flats. Mossman stands to make a fortune. In a way it's quite handy for us. It's a lot shorter distance than before.'

'I guess Mossman must still own the Half-Box,' Conrad mused, 'otherwise why would Rickard have retained the M? I'd have thought someone like Rickard would pretty soon have changed the M to an R.'

Lowell leaned forward. Conrad's words had hit him like a douche of cold water. It was so obvious too. Why had he not realized before the significance of that one letter?

'The M in Half-Box M refers to Mossman?' he said.

'Yeah. He only signed it over to Rickard when he

got his hands on the old stage line.'

'The line that was originally scheduled to run to Buckhorn?'

'That's it. The old place never recovered. It's nothing now but a ghost town.' Conrad suddenly stopped. 'Sorry,' he said. 'Of course, you'd know that.'

There was an anxious look on Fuller's face. He glanced at Eliot.

'Mr Lowell might not want to talk about events in Buckhorn,' he said. 'It can't have been easy to see the place die.'

Lowell felt a stab of pain at Fuller's words, which had a significance beyond his intended meaning. Fuller did not know the irony they contained. For a moment he felt like moving away and then something seemed to be released inside him. It was almost a physical feeling and he felt not only able to speak, but an urge to do so.

'It's all right,' he said. 'There's no need for awkwardness.' He paused for just a moment while the others looked closely at him.

'There was a fire in Buckhorn', he continued. 'I think you know that. People got badly hurt. People died. One of them was my wife.'

It was only once he had spoken the words that he realized their full import. It wasn't just the blunt statement of fact. It was that he had never been able to talk of it before. He was surprised at the way he felt. There was still pain, but there was also a sense of relief, of a weight having been lifted from his shoulders.

'I'm sorry,' Fuller said. 'None of us knew.'

There was silence for a moment, during which Lowell was thinking hard. Having been released from the burden of his secret, he wanted to leave it behind. There was no point in dwelling on it now, and he wanted to prevent an atmosphere of embarrassment from developing.

'Tell me,' he said, turning to Fuller. 'What else do you know about Mossman?'

'Nothin' much. He spent most of his time at the Half-Box. He never came to town. You could ask anybody in Granton and I reckon they'd say the same thing. He was always somethin' of a mystery. There was some talk about the manner in which he got his hands on the stage line. Funny, Dinsdale was involved in that negotiation too.'

'Dinsdale! He sure seems to have some dubious clients.'

'People thought that once he'd got control of the stage company, they'd see more of Mossman. But the next thing we heard was that he'd built the rail-line to Shoshone Flats. I guess that's where he is now, although nobody knows for sure.'

Lowell was thinking hard. Since his wife died in the fire and he had withdrawn from the world, he had barely thought about those events. It had been too painful. Now he was beginning to wonder whether he hadn't missed something quite obvious, in the same way as he had failed to see any significance in the letter M in the name of Rickard's ranch. He looked at the others who were watching him intently.

'What is it?' Eliot asked.

'That fire,' Lowell said. 'Maybe it wasn't an accident. Maybe it was started deliberately.'

It had only just occurred to him and he expected them to raise objections, but to his surprise they didn't seem to react in that way to his suggestion.

'Mossman certainly benefited from that fire,' Fuller said. 'It was the final nail in the coffin for Buckhorn as a goin' concern.' He glanced at Lowell, concerned that he might have used the wrong words, but Lowell didn't seem to notice.

'I remember there was some speculation about the causes of the fire,' Eliot said, 'but it was only talk.'

'There's one way to find out,' Lowell said.

'What do you mean?' Conrad asked.

'You say Dinsdale was involved in the deal for the stage line. Now he's Rickard's lawyer. The way I see it, he's likely to know the answers.' He turned to Fuller. 'Do you reckon you could spare me for a while?' he said.

'Sure. The roundup's just about complete. We're almost ready to go.'

'What are you plannin' to do?' Eliot asked.

'Pay a visit to Dinsdale.'

'You'd be headin' straight back into the firin' line,' Eliot replied. Fuller shrugged. 'You've got the marshal to worry about as well. At least let me come with you this time.'

'I don't intend wastin' time,' Lowell replied. He glanced towards Fuller.

'Eliot's right. I can spare a couple of hands,' Fuller said. He poured the last of the whiskey into their glasses. 'Just make sure you get back in one piece. I'll be needin' everyone for the trail drive.'

They were about to call it a night. Conrad stood up to go down the veranda steps when the door to the ranch-house opened and Lorna appeared.

'Have you boys not finished yet?' she said. 'I was wondering if you might like a bite of supper.'

'Thank you, ma'am,' Conrad said, 'but I think I'll call it a day.'

He was about to go when Fuller put a detaining hand on his arm.

'Actually, Conrad,' he said, 'Could you stick

around for a few minutes. Now that Lorna's here there's a word I need to have with you all.'

Lorna looked her uncle. 'That sounds ominous,' she said.

'Pull up a chair, Lorna,' Fuller replied. 'This does concern you.'

Lorna took Conrad's vacant seat while the foreman leaned on the balcony rail.

'You can probably guess what I'm gonna say. I'm worried about leavin' you here. I know we've agreed already that if Rickard launches an attack, it's much more likely to be on the herd. However, I wouldn't feel comfortable leavin' you behind.'

'There'll still be people around,' Conrad said.

'Yeah, but even so I don't like the idea of Lorna being exposed to any danger.'

'Fuller's right,' Lowell said.

Fuller turned to Lorna. 'I think it best that while we're away, you move into town and stay with one of the neighbours. I know the Dawsons would be happy to have you. Or you might prefer to choose some of your own friends.'

Lorna sat in silence for a few moments. Lowell was looking at her but he couldn't decipher the look on her features.

'That's very thoughtful of you, uncle,' she eventually replied. 'I really do appreciate your concern.

But I have no intention of moving to town.'

'Like your uncle says, it wouldn't be safe leavin' you here.'

'I don't intend stayin' at the Long Rail either. Since I came here, I've tried to take an interest in the affairs of the ranch. Well, now the time's come for me to experience a trail drive at first hand. In fact, it will be an invaluable addition to my education. I'm coming with you.'

'You can't do that!' Fuller said. He looked at the others for support.

'And why not? I'm a good rider. I can rough it.'

'It ain't no kinda life for a girl,' Fuller said.

'I'm not a girl. I'm a woman full grown. Now, it's no use arguing. I've made up my mind.' Fuller seemed to be searching for words but before he could say anything more Lorna added: 'And there's one other thing. I can cook.'

There was a moment's silence and then Conrad laughed.

'She's got you there,' he said.

'I've got a cook,' Fuller said, but he was struggling. He sensed that on this occasion Lorna was inflexible. What she said was true. She had grown into womanhood and he had barely noticed it. He had tended to try and shelter her from some of the rougher elements of life on the ranch, but he saw that it was neither necessary nor appropriate any more.

'Well,' she said, 'that's settled then.'

She turned and walked away. There was no further mention of supper and Lowell wondered whether her arrival might have had less to do with supper and more to do with timing the announcement of her determination to accompany the trail drive. If so, Fuller had been pretty cleverly manipulated. It was true what Eliot had said: she was quite a woman.

'Guess I'll be turnin' in too,' Fuller said.

They all got to their feet to make their departure. As he made his way back to the bunkhouse, Lowell's thoughts were on Mossman. He didn't intend coming away from his visit to Dinsdale without having some answers.

CHAPTER FOUR

Early the following morning Lowell and Eliot set off for Granton. Lowell was on edge and they covered the ground as quickly as they could. When they reached town they drew to a halt outside the lawyer's office and fastened their horses to the nearest hitch-rack.

'Want me to come in with you?' Eliot said.

'Nope. I'll deal with Dinsdale my way.'

'Take it easy,' Eliot replied. 'Don't go doin' anythin' hasty.'

'Don't worry about me.'

Lowell glanced around. The Fashion Restaurant was a little further up the street.

'Wait there,' Lowell said. 'This shouldn't take too long. In fact you can order me a coffee and flapjacks.'

'I'll watch out for Marshal Fowler,' Eliot replied.

Lowell turned and walked through the door of the building. Inside there was a gloomy lobby not unlike Rickard's outer office. It was no young woman sitting behind the desk but an ugly looking man with a growth of bristle lining his chin. As Lowell advanced into the room his hand dropped below the level of the desk. Lowell wasn't taking any chances. In an instant he had whipped out his gun.

'I'm lookin' for Dinsdale,' he said.

'Mr Dinsdale ain't here.'

The words had a familiar ring but Lowell wasn't going to be deterred. Ignoring the man, he strode to a door to the left of the desk. As he did so the man made a sudden move and Lowell brought his gun down on the man's head. With a moan he sank to the floor. There was a sound of movement from behind the door. Lowell kicked at it and it flew open to reveal the cringing form of the lawyer standing by a window. Beyond him, Lowell saw movement in the street outside.

'What is this?' Dinsdale began. 'You have no right—' His words were choked off as Lowell grabbed him by the throat.

'I want answers,' he snapped, 'and I don't intend beatin' about the bush.'

'I'm not in a position to divulge. . . .' The lawyer broke off again as a light of recognition suddenly dawned in his eyes.

'If this is about the proposed sale of the Long Rail, you will have to talk to Mr Rickard.'

'I intend dealin' with Rickard. But first of all I want to know about Mossman.'

Lowell had relaxed his hold on Dinsdale but the lawyer remained pressed against the wall.

'Mossman?' he repeated questioningly. 'Mossman?'

'Don't pretend you don't know who Mossman is.'

Dinsdale quickly sensed that there was no point in dissembling. Probably most people in Granton had heard the name.

'I may have acted for Mossman in the past,' he mumbled. 'But that was long ago.'

'You're lyin',' Lowell said. 'Now don't misunderstand me. I ain't foolin'. I'll give you one more chance to tell me all you know about Mossman.'

'I don't know anything. As I say, I haven't had contact with Mossman for a long time.'

Lowell had put his gun back in its holster. Now he withdrew it and held it in the lawyer's face.

'You wouldn't. . . .' he began, but got no further as Lowell drove the barrel of the gun into the lawyer's stomach. He doubled over and would have sunk to the floor but for Lowell's supporting arm.

'Who started the fire?' he said.

The lawyer looked at him through glazed eyes.

'Who started the fire?' Lowell said again.

'What fire?' he managed to say. 'I don't know what you're talkin' about.'

Lowell swung his fist and the lawyer's nose burst open like a ripened fruit. Blood poured down his face.

'You know which fire. The fire that burned down part of Buckhorn. The fire that killed my wife.'

Lowell was enraged now. As the lawyer swayed, he banged his head against the wall. Dinsdale groaned. He was gasping for breath and was close to unconsciousness. Lowell raised his gun again.

'I had nothing to do with it,' the lawyer said. 'It was Mossman's idea.'

'Because he wanted that stage line? It was due to link with Buckhorn.' Lowell had a sudden inspiration. 'Who else died in that fire?' he said.

'Rogers. He had the original bid.'

It was all becoming clear now to Lowell. 'Where is Mossman now?'

'He moved away to Shoshone Flats.'

'I know that. Where in Shoshone Flats?'

'Really, I don't know. Please don't kill me.'

The rage suddenly died in Lowell. He glanced around the lawyer's office. There was a safe in one corner. Seizing the flagging Dinsdale, he dragged him to it.

'Open the safe,' he said.

Dinsdale was beyond offering any objection. He turned the combination and the safe swung open. Lowell released his hold on him and he fell to his knees. Lowell looked inside the safe. There were a number of papers and he didn't feel like sifting through them. Instead, he gathered them all up and thrust the bundle inside his jacket. Dinsdale was making strange whimpering noises and retching. A trail of blood led from the window to the safe and gathered in two pools. Lowell looked for a moment on the battered figure of the lawyer and then strode to the door. The other man still lay on the floor, breathing shallowly. Lowell stepped over him and made for the outer door.

As he stepped outside, the sunlight hit him like an explosion. He stood for a few moments before beginning to make his way to the Fashion Restaurant but he hadn't gone more than a few paces when a shot rang out, whistling just past his shoulder. He assumed that it came from the lawyer's office and turned quickly to face his attacker. The movement was enough to save him

86

from a second bullet which tugged at the sleeve of his jacket. Instantly he flung himself to the ground and rolled to the edge of the boardwalk. Someone was screaming and people were running in different directions. Shots were being fired from several different points and he realised he was under fire from more than one gunman.

Bullets tore up the dust in front of him. He saw a stab of flame coming from the direction of an alleyway and returned fire. At the same moment, from the corner of his eye, he saw movement to his left and swinging his gun in that direction, he loosed off a couple of shots. There was a scream and then a man toppled forward from behind a stanchion, landing in the road with a dull crash. Taking a chance, Lowell sprang to his feet and ran doubled over to the doorway of a store which offered better protection. A bullet thudded into the wall nearby and then a salvo of shots shattered the window and sent shards of glass raining down on him. As his eyes searched the street, a shot rang out from the direction of the Fashion Restaurant and he caught a glimpse of Eliot just inside the doorway.

'Lowell!' he called. 'Are you OK?'

'Yeah. Can you see anything?'

'No, but I think I got one of 'em.'

Lowell grinned. Whoever the attackers were, that meant two of them were accounted for. Suddenly he realized that the gunfire had ceased. A strange silence seemed to envelope the town. It hung in the air like something palpable and then through it he heard the sound of someone running. For a moment he considered chasing him, but he couldn't see anyone and the sounds quickly receded. The silence continued till it was broken by the sound of hoof beats. Lowell leaned out and down the street two horsemen appeared, riding hard.

He realized what had happened. The gunnies had been surprised by Eliot's appearance on the scene and had decided to call it a day. They were making their getaway but coming in his direction. The horses were kicking up a lot of dust but as they got close Lowell recognized Vernon by the buckskin jacket he was wearing. Even as he realized who it was there was a shot from the Fashion Restaurant and the other gunman fell backwards from his horse. Vernon strove to control his mount as it reared into the air, kicking its legs and almost falling backwards. For a few seconds he clung on, fighting hard to gain control, but the spooked horse kept bucking and he fell to the ground, narrowly avoiding the horse's flailing hoofs. At the same moment Lowell stepped from his cover into the glare of the street. Vernon struggled to his feet and stood immobile, staring at the grimly advancing figure.

'I don't know who you are or what this is about,' Lowell said, 'but I'm gonna give you a fair chance.' Vernon shrank back.

'It was Rickard,' he sobbed. 'He's the one you really want. I had no choice. I didn't want any part of it but he made me.'

'You didn't want any part in what?'

'It was Rickard. I don't ask questions. It was Rickard's orders. There was nothin' I could do.'

Lowell's advance was inexorable. His eyes were focused on his adversary, but he was aware that people had re-emerged from shelter and were standing on the boardwalks, watching intently. There was no movement. Silence had returned and continued to hold sway, an unnatural silence thick with tension. When he was satisfied that he was at an appropriate distance, he halted and stood in his tracks. Vernon continued to move away till Lowell rapped out:

'That's far enough.'

Vernon had stopped talking and was looking about him agitatedly. He was breathing heavily and licking his lips.

'All right,' Lowell rapped. 'I've heard enough. The time for talk is over. Now, go for your gun.'

Vernon looked about him one more time, as if appealing to the spectators to do something and come to his rescue. He was met with a blank wall of indifference. Then he turned towards Lowell. He had begun to shake and beads of sweat ran down his cheeks.

'You've got this wrong,' he bleated.

Suddenly, his hand dropped towards his holster. The movement was quick and his gun was in his hand in an instant. Before he could squeeze the trigger, however, Lowell's gun had spoken and Vernon reeled backwards as a bullet tore into his chest. He raised his gun again but Lowell's second bullet had already ripped through his throat. Gurgling and coughing, he sank to the ground, twitching. Lowell placed his gun back in its holster and turned away from the dying man. The silence, shattered by the explosion of gunfire, was broken now by the murmur of voices and the movement of people. Lowell felt a hand on his arm and turned to see Eliot.

'I reckon we'd better get out of here,' he said. 'I figure we ain't gonna get much sympathy from the marshal.'

Quickly they made their way to their horses and

swung into leather. A crowd had gathered beside Vernon's lifeless body and a few of them began to move in their direction. Eliot paused for just a moment.

'It's a pity about those flapjacks,' he said.

'Maybe another time,' Lowell replied.

Spurring their horses, they turned away from the scene of activity and began to ride down the street. Lowell glanced over his shoulder, looking for the marshal, but there was no sign of him. They gathered speed and in a matter of minutes had left the town behind them and were clear.

They carried on riding till they were confident that they were safe from pursuit, when they drew to a halt.

'Well,' Eliot said. 'What happened back there? I heard the shootin' but I didn't realize at first that it was you they were shootin' at.'

'The man I shot,' Lowell replied. 'I don't know who he is, but I had a spot of trouble with him before. The way I figure it, he was hired to kill me.'

'Who would do that?'

'The same person tried to get me killed last time. I figured it was Rickard but now I'm not so sure.'

'You ain't thinkin' it might have been Mossman? Did you find out anythin', by the way?'

'Yes. It was Mossman started that fire. That's one

reason why I figure he might be behind it all. You see, I was marshal at that time. I was pretty much involved in the campaign to get the stage-line to run to Buckhorn.'

'Would that be enough to account for it though? Especially after this amount of time's gone by.'

'That's the bit I don't understand,' Lowell replied. 'Assumin' Mossman is the really the one who wants me dead, why has he waited till now?'

'You're sure it was Mossman who started the fire?'

'I'm sure. I should have realized it before now. Guess I didn't like to think about it.'

Eliot seemed to weigh up what Lowell had said, and then he suddenly gave a loud whistle.

'Of course,' he said. 'Hell, it's obvious!'

Lowell responded with a puzzled look. 'What's obvious?' he said.

'I know this is maybe painful for you, but did many people die in that fire?'

'A few,' Lowell replied.

'Were they all accounted for? I mean, were they all identified?'

Lowell's face was drawn. 'Not all,' he answered.

'And you were right there, fightin' the fire?'

Lowell seemed to make a conscious effort to reply. 'Yes. I got burned myself.' He hesitated.

'Tryin' to rescue Ella,' he concluded.

'Then there's your answer. Mossman must have assumed that you died too. He thought you were one of the victims. It's taken him till now to realize that you survived. Hell, you've been livin' like a hermit in that damned old ghost town. We only saw you in Granton when you came in from time to time for supplies. He's probably not the only one to have made the same assumption.'

Lowell was silent for a few moments and when he looked at Eliot his expression had changed. It was still grim but there was a dawning light of understanding in it.

'Somethin' must have happened to make Mossman realize he was wrong, that you didn't perish in the fire,' Eliot continued. 'It doesn't matter what. Maybe somebody he knows recognized you and word filtered back. Whatever it was, he figured you were a danger. He wasn't to know how much you knew or whether or not you suspected him, but once he realized you were alive, his security was ended. He wants you dead, this time for sure.'

Lowell slowly nodded. 'I reckon you're right,' he said. 'It adds up.' He reached into his jacket pocket and brought out the papers he had removed.

'There might be more answers here,' he said. 'I

took them from Dinsdale's safe. I figure there could be enough to put him and Rickard behind bars, but maybe there's somethin' about Mossman too.'

They sat their horses for a time, mulling things over but not saying much. Finally Eliot turned to Lowell.

'Come on,' he said. 'Let's ride. We can talk things over later.'

After they got back to the Long Rail, Lowell took the first opportunity that presented itself to look through the papers, but he was disappointed. So far as he could make out, they were mostly legal documents referring to a variety of matters not connected with either Rickard or Mossman. Fuller had given him the use of his study, and he sat up into the early hours. He was about to call it a day when he heard the soft tread of feet and looked up to see Lorna standing in the doorway.

'I hope I didn't startle you,' she said. 'I couldn't sleep. I saw the lamplight and wondered how you were getting on.'

Lowell was taken by surprise. He hadn't expected anyone else to still be awake, least of all Lorna. He felt flustered and unsure of his ground.

'My uncle used to keep things from me, but not anymore,' she said. 'To be honest, I would have

94

had to be stupid not to know what was going on.'

Lowell didn't question how much she knew. That was between her and Fuller. She came into the room and sat beside him. She was still dressed in her normal attire, and Lowell wondered if she had been awake all night. He felt disturbed by her proximity.

'I've been lookin' through these papers, but they don't make much sense to me,' he said. 'I think I'm out of my depth. I don't understand legal language. I'm not even sure what I'm lookin' for.'

She looked at the pile of papers littering the desk. 'Would you mind if I take a look?' she said.

'No. You're welcome.'

She leaned over and sifted through them, lifting one and then another to give it a quick glance. He glanced at her face in profile and breathed in the fragrance of her perfume.

'I tell you what,' she said. 'You must be exhausted. Why don't you get some rest while I take more time to examine them?'

He didn't want to leave her but at the same time he appreciated the excuse to do so. After everything that he had been through, it was true he was feeling tired and what she said made sense.

'Are you sure you wouldn't mind?' he said.

'I wouldn't have offered if I did,' she replied.

She smiled and placed a hand on his arm.

'Go on. You'll have to be back in the saddle soon. Get some rest while you can. I can't sleep anyway. Maybe I'll have more luck than you.'

Lowell reluctantly got to his feet and made his way to the door where he turned back to take a final look at her sitting in the lamplight.

'Thanks,' he said. 'I sure appreciate your help.'

He turned and left her, making his way through the darkness outside back to the bunkhouse.

Rickard didn't shed any tears either over Vernon's demise or over what had happened to Dinsdale. The stolen papers, however, were a different matter. He didn't know exactly what papers had been taken or what was in them, but he was astute enough to know they might contain incriminating material. Some people had seen Lowell ride off in the company of Eliot and he had it on good report that Eliot's horse was carrying a Long Rail brand. This only confirmed what his gunslicks had told him following the Buckhorn incident; that they had followed the sign of two men in the general direction of the Long Rail. He was pretty sure that Lowell had somehow ended up there. There was only one logical conclusion. He could no longer delay his assault on the Long Rail. In a way things had turned out quite well. He now had the opportunity to deal with both Fuller and Lowell together. At the same time, he would be carrying out Mossman's instructions and so have nothing further to fear from that quarter. He was still puzzled to know what Mossman had against Lowell, but it didn't much matter now.

He sat at his desk thinking these things over before eventually getting to his feet and walking to the window. For a few minutes he stood looking out over the main street. It was quiet enough now, but he had a sudden vision of how it might be if Lowell were to show up again. Maybe Vernon's fate would be his next time, or even worse. After all, Lowell had already paid one visit to his sanctum. Turning away from the window, he walked across the room and out the door. His secretary looked up at his appearance. He regarded her for a few moments. She was very attractive. She didn't do much. Maybe it was time to make better use of her attributes. That was something to think about, but for the moment he had other concerns.

'I may be gone for some time,' he said. She gave him an enquiring look. 'I have some business to attend to back at the ranch,' he continued 'but I think I may safely leave you to look after things here.'

'Of course,' she said. 'How long will you be away?'

'I don't know. Not too long.' She smiled and he leaned slightly in her direction.

'How do you find your duties here?' he said. She didn't reply immediately and he continued. 'You do a very good job. Don't think I haven't noticed or appreciated your work here or the contribution you make to the smooth running of the business. How would you feel about taking on more respon-sibility? Of course, any additional duties you might assume would be more than adequately compen-sated.'

'Thank you, Mr Rickard,' she said.

He bent lower and then straightened up again. 'That's settled then,' he said. 'We can talk further when I get back.'

He gave an awkward smiled and made for the stairs. The secretary listened to his footsteps and when the outer door closed, adjusted her skirt, observed her nails and opened the pages of a mag-azine.

The last of the cattle had been rounded up and trail branded. They were ready for the drive. Conrad had mixed a few old bulls with the herd to set a steady pace and exert a calming influence. His intention was to drive the herd hard, at least during the early stages of the drive, and tire the cattle so that when they were bedded down for the night they would be too weary to attempt to bolt. In the early morning, before dawn, they started out. Fuller rode at the head of the herd, with Eliot and Lowell riding point on either side. Conrad had a more general role, acting as trouble-shooter and guide, riding up and down the line, looking out for points of strain or stress, riding ahead to look out for good grass and bedding ground. Right at the rear came the chuck-wagon, with Lorna riding alongside the cook.

Almost from the start the drag rider had to apply his whip to encourage some of the trailing cows, being careful at the same time not to crowd them. At the start, a lot of cattle were inclined to be difficult but Conrad was confident that they would soon settle down. The herd was strung out for about half a mile; they travelled slowly, leaving the Long Rail behind them.

The men had been warned right from the start that there might be trouble and they were prepared to meet it if it arose. Fuller had no doubts about their commitment. Most of them had worked for him for a long time and they were all loyal to the brand. His main concern was Lorna.

He felt she had somehow outmanoeuvred him. He would certainly have felt happier if she were back in Granton. Conrad, for the moment, was riding alongside him, and he felt a need to voice his doubts.

'It maybe isn't ideal,' Conrad said, 'but look at it this way. Would she have been very much safer if you had left her in Granton? Rickard has a lot of influence. If he's got it in for the Long Rail, it might not have been the best place for her to be.'

'He wouldn't. . . .' Fuller began, but a moment's reflection was enough to remind him that Rickard was probably capable of anything. 'You've got a point there,' he conceded. 'I hadn't looked at it like that.'

'At least this way we can keep an eye on her ourselves. She'll be safe enough.'

Conrad's words helped calm Fuller's fears. He felt a lot better. He certainly had no worries about Lorna's abilities to last the course. She was young, strong and toughened by her time out west. She was a fine rider and good with horses. In fact, she might prove really useful with the remuda. All in all, maybe it wasn't such bad thing to have her along.

They carried on riding till noon, when the cattle were halted and allowed to graze. Conrad wanted to push on fast so before long they were on the trail once more, continuing till the sun began to sink. Then the men started to work the cattle into a more compact space, circling round them till within a short period of time they were all nicely bedded down. They had to be watched throughout the night, and the men took it in turns to do a shift of about two hours. Eliot and Lowell took the cocktail watch, the last watch before daylight. As they circled the herd they murmured softly to soothe the cattle and when they crossed, they pulled their horses to a halt.

'So far, so good,' Eliot said.

'Yeah. We've made a start.'

Lowell looked about. It was a clear starry night. The resting herd seemed contented. Away to their left a light shone where the cook had hung a lantern on the boom of the chuck wagon, inside of which, probably sleeping, was Lorna Fuller.

'You know,' he said. 'I haven't felt so good in a long time.'

'Rickard might have somethin' to say about that,' Eliot remarked.

'He can come whenever he wants. We're ready for him.'

The first day set the pattern for the ones that followed. Early in the morning the men made their way to the chuck-wagon and had breakfast while the wrangler went out to drive in the horses. Lorna proved Fuller right, making herself useful by helping the wrangler bring them in and taking an inventory of them by name and colour to make sure none were missing. The men roped and saddled new mounts.

When everything was ready, the cattle were thrown off their pasturage and set in motion till noon when they were allowed to drink and graze. Some of the men changed their horses. Late in the afternoon the cattle were driven another few miles before being allowed to graze again until night fell, when they were put on the next bedding ground. The herd was becoming trail-broken. Once they were moving, they carried on with little need for close supervision, their heads swaying to the steady rhythm of the pace they set. The cowhands lounged in their saddles. One bull had established himself as leader of the herd, an old mossback with drooping scaly horns, clipped and broken from fighting. Every morning, when the herd was starting out, he was pointed in the direction Fuller wanted to go, towards the railhead at Shoshone Flats.

Lowell had plenty to keep him occupied, but as they progressed he began to think more and more about what he would do once he got there. Since he had learned that Mossman was responsible for the fire that had killed his wife, his thirst for revenge had become all consuming. Once the trail drive was over, he intended to find Mossman. Other than that Mossman was living somewhere in the vicinity of Shoshone Flats, he didn't know exactly where he was to be found. No one seemed to know much about him. He himself had not seen him more than a couple of times. That had been quite a long time ago and he wasn't even certain he would recognize him. It seemed like Mossman went out of his way to court obscurity. Was his elusiveness just a way of preserving his anonymity or was there something more to it? During the course of his rise to power, he must have upset plenty of people. Maybe it was just a way of keeping his enemies at arm's length, of staying alive. As far as Lowell was concerned, his time of security was over.

Rickard had been giving thought to launching an all-out assault on the Long Rail, but when his spies reported that Fuller had started on the trail drive his mind was made up. It would be easier to attack him while he was on the move. When he had dealt with him, he could take over the herd and incorporate it into his own before starting up the trail himself. The question he now had to consider was where to deliver the attack. Since the weight of numbers was heavily on his side and he had employed some of the fastest guns for hire, it probably didn't make a lot of difference. Still, it was only sensible to take the terrain into account. He knew the country between Granton and Shoshone Flats a little himself, but some of his ranch-hands knew it a lot better. Summoning one of them, an oldster by name of Bennett, to his office, he broached the matter.

'There's a few places along the trail might be suitable,' he replied. 'Yes, quite a few.' He paused, rubbing his grizzled chin.

'Let me see. There's the river. That might be a good place. Catch 'em while they're tryin' to get across. But it ain't that wide. There's one or two other places they might get held up.'

'Never mind goin' though the whole shebang,' Rickard snapped. 'Just tell me what's the best place.'

'Well, if you're figurin' to take over those cow critters, you might want to save yourself the bother of havin' to drive 'em all the way back from Shoshone Flats. On the other hand. . . .'

'I'm beginnin' to lose patience,' Rickard snapped.

104

Bennett looked at him with a grin on his face.

'I got just the spot,' he said. 'Yes, just the right spot. Count on it. Fuller won't know what's hit him.'

CHAPTER FIVE

Conrad, having ridden ahead, surveyed the herd from the summit of a rising crest of land flanked on either side by high outcrops of rock. It was stretched out in a long sinuous line like an extended column of ants. So far they had met with only minor difficulties, but he foresaw more serious problems in getting the cattle through the narrow defile. They would have their work cut out to keep them in order. The ground was more broken and it would be essential to keep them from getting too close to the rocks. But it wasn't the difficulties of the terrain that most worried him. For some time there had been a thick, muffled feeling to the air and he knew it presaged a storm. Dark clouds had blown up and on the horizon he saw the first flicker of lightning. The heaviness in the atmosphere was replaced by a growing wind as squalls came streaking towards him across the prairie. He rose in his stirrups and looked back once more at the herd. The column was slowly approaching. After watching it for a little longer, he spurred his horse and rode on, looking for the nearest good place to bed the cattle once they had got through the gorge.

Conrad wasn't the only one watching. Concealed behind the rocks and granite outcrops on either side of the trail was Rickard and his gang. As Conrad rode away, one of the gunnies raised his rifle and drew a bead on his back. A moment later the rifle was knocked out of his hand by Rickard.

'What the hell do you think you're doin'?' he snapped. 'If you'd taken a shot, Fuller would have been warned. You might have blown the whole show.'

'I coulda had him. He was an easy target.'

'He's out of range. If you try and pull a stunt like that once more. . . .'

'I'm sorry, boss. It won't happen again.'

Rickard struggled to contain his anger. The men nearby were watching the outcome closely. Rickard turned on them.

'Keep your eyes on the trail,' he said.

He looked hard at the offending gunman once

more and then stomped off.

He wasn't in the best frame of mind and was feeling hot and uncomfortable. The air had grown heavy and it seemed almost an effort to breathe. There was a tense expectancy in the atmosphere which wasn't just to do with waiting for the herd to arrive. It was unfortunate, because the ride itself had been easy. There was no question about the route Fuller had to follow. The cattle trail was a familiar one. It was just a matter of getting on ahead of the herd and taking up position without being spotted. Fuller was no fool. He would anticipate the possibility of an attack and he would be careful to keep an eye out for trouble. It had not been an easy matter to avoid detection. A big group of riders kicked up a lot of dust. It had been an exhausting experience but now they had arrived at the place Bennett had selected he was satisfied. The oldster was right. It was a good spot. He had been a little worried when he saw Conrad riding ahead of the herd in case he detected something, but they had come from a different direction and taken care to leave their horses at a little distance. He felt a resurgence of anger when he thought again of the fact that one loose shot could have jeopardized the whole thing. But the danger was past. All they had to do now was to sit and wait till

Fuller and the rest of his Long Rail cowboys fell right into the trap he had prepared.

When he had taken his place high among the rocks, he looked out over the landscape. Far off he could just make out the course of the river Fuller would have to cross. He had considered making that his point of attack, but as Bennett had indicated, the river was not much of an obstacle. It was little more than a stream. Besides, it would have been difficult to make an approach without being detected. He had also considered a night attack but had rejected that idea too. Fuller would probably expect it and make appropriate arrangements. In the darkness, anything could happen. Things could get out of hand. No, this way he had control of the situation. Fuller was riding straight into a deadly ambush. He would be taken by surprise and he would be routed.

At the same time, his choice of cover was a fair guarantee of his own safety. He certainly didn't intend getting involved with any shooting. That was what he employed men for, men who were accustomed to using a gun. With a grin replacing the scowl on his face, he licked his lips in anticipation. It was then that he spotted something he hadn't noticed because it had been concealed by an outcrop of rock and was coming from a direction other than the river; in fact from the direction of Granton. His grin fell away immediately. What was it? The last thing he wanted was any extraneous element over which he had no control risking his plans. He reached into a bundle lying beside him on the ground and, pulling out his field-glasses, put them to his eyes. For a few moments the lenses roved over the waving field of buffalo and gamma grass before focusing on the distant object. Rickard gave a curse. It was the mule-train carrying his own store of hides to Shoshone Flats.

Lowell and Eliot were riding close to the herd and the swing men were doing the same. The gathering storm was making the cattle restless. The clouds which had gathered slowly now piled and mushroomed. The air was dark and the rumble of thunder below the horizon was getting closer. As if that wasn't enough, the going was more difficult. The land sloped upwards and the cattle felt the resistance. The ground was rockier and hurt their hoofs. Lowell's eyes, searching the terrain, saw for the first time something else which was making them uneasy. It was the mule train. Even from a distance his nostrils picked up the faint rank smell of animal hides. Just at that moment Fuller rode up to him.

'This storm ain't good,' he said.

'Yeah. There's another thing too. Look over there.' He pointed out the distant line of mules and wagons. 'The cows must be pickin' up the scent.'

Suddenly he had an inspiration. There was only one man trading in buffalo hides. The mule train must be Rickard's. One thought followed another. Where else would they be going but to the rail-head at Shoshone Flats. And who would Rickard be dealing with? There was no way of knowing for sure, but there was a good chance it was Mossman. In which case, maybe whoever was driving the mule train might know where Mossman was to be found.

'Don't let any of the critters get out of line,' Fuller said. 'This is about the last thing we could have done with.'

Lowell nodded and Fuller began to ride back towards the head of the herd. Lowell glanced over his shoulder towards the mule train and then directed his attention back to the job in hand. A few of the cows were striving to break loose and he rode up close to turn them back. Some of the cattle were bellowing and bawling and an electric glow flickered along their horns. He had a sudden concern that the iron wheel rims on the chuck-wagon in which Lorna was riding might attract the lightning, but there was nothing he could do about it. The wind had risen to a howling gale and he hunkered down into his slicker as a fork of white fire flashed between the clouds. A thunderclap boomed and before Lowell or anyone else had time to do anything to prevent it, the herd suddenly began to run.

In an instant he had spurred his horse and was riding alongside the terrified steers. There was a clacking of horns as some of them collided and fell, making a jumble of bodies. The thunder in the heavens was answered by the thunder of hoofs as the roiling sea of cattle lunged on in a blind panic. The clouds opened and rain descended like a curtain. Fast as the cattle were running, his horse was going quicker and he began to get alongside the lead animals. Drawing his gun, he fired into the air in an attempt to get the leaders to swing in the hope that the following cattle would follow and they would circle. Fuller and his men were experienced cow-hands. They knew what had to be done and worked together like clockwork. As they struggled to gain control, they continued to make as much noise as they could; shouting, yelling, cussing and firing their guns. They were gradually forcing the lead cattle to turn and the herd was beginning to mill. If they could keep it up, the cattle would gradually exhaust themselves.

Lowell urged his horse as close to the herd as he dared, now using his slicker as a flail to smash into the faces if the foremost steers. It seemed to be going well when suddenly he became aware of an increased level of shooting. He felt the close-packed animals begin to yield and a group of demented steers broke away, charging off across the sodden prairie. Instinctively he turned his horse to pursue them and saw a body of riders pouring down on them from the direction of the rocky plateau. Bullets were whining through the air over his head and for just a few moments he thought they were loose shots from some of Fuller's men. Then, when he managed to take a closer look, he realized that the newcomers were not Long Rail riders. He still didn't realize what was happening, but a bullet that ricocheted from the horn of his saddle told him that whatever it was, he was in a fight for his life.

In the heat of the moment, he had allowed himself to get ahead of the breakaway group which was coming up rapidly behind him. A new hazard presented itself. If he didn't manage to get out of their way, he was in danger of being trampled. His horse was already tiring and he couldn't hope to stay ahead for long. The leaders were upon him and he was quickly in the midst of them. His attention now was focused simply on keeping his horse from falling. If it was to put its leg into a prairie dog hole or some other obstacle it would spell disaster. There was no way he would be able to avoid the thundering hoofs. His best chance was to try and edge his way out of the heaving mass of cattle, and when he saw a gap he guided the sorrel into it. Gradually the breakaway herd began to string out as the fastest animals forged ahead and he was able to steer his horse out of the press of the frenzied beasts. He slowed down, watching the cattle stream by. There was nothing he could do to stop them. The only thing to do was to let them run on as long as their endurance lasted. He had more urgent matters to attend to.

Through the driving rain he could see that a melee had developed at the point at which the cows he had been following had broken away. It was only then that he realized that the attack from Rickard had arrived. Turning his horse, he began to ride back.

He rode as hard as his flagging mount permitted towards the heart of the struggle that was taking place between Fuller's Long Rail cowboys and Rickard's gang of gunslicks. Isolated groups of cattle passed him and to his right he could see the main body of the herd as it continued its headlong chase. Cattle were straggling across a wide area and as he rode he was still partly thinking about how difficult a job it would be to round them up again. Then he had another thought. He had been so caught up with the stampede that he had forgotten about Lorna. Suddenly her image flashed across his mind. What had happened to her? Was she still safe with the chuck-wagon? A fresh wave of fury swept over him. If Rickard's men had hurt her. . . . Like a man possessed he rode into the heart of the battle.

Even as he approached the melee, groups of riders began to break apart and form separate struggles within the main battle. He found himself facing an oncoming rider. Touching the horse's flanks with his spurs, he drew it to one side and pressed the trigger of his Winchester. The man flung up his arms and fell backwards over his horse. Another rider appeared; holding his rifle with one hand, he squeezed off another shot and the man fell away to the side. His foot caught in the stirrups and prevented him from falling cleanly. Lowell heard the man's screams above the tumult of the battle as he was dragged across the sodden ground. As he turned his mount, his horse reared as another bullet scorched its flank. Lowell was almost thrown, but he managed to bring the animal back under control. The movement shook the rifle from his grasp. Reaching for one of his six-guns, he began to blaze away at the mass of struggling horsemen in front of him, but quickly realized that he was taking a risk of hitting one of his own men.

In the driving rain, it was hard to see what was happening. Darkness hung over the prairie and thunder continued to roll around the sky. A vivid flash of lightning lit up the scene and in that instant Lowell had a sharply etched vision of something almost unreal, like a visual parable of everything his life had become since the death of his wife. For some reason, he thought of Lorna's print on the wall of the room in which he had found himself recuperating from his injury back at the Long Rail. It was only momentary; he was jerked back to reality as a bullet whined close by and he quickly jammed more slugs into his six-gun. Out of the melange of men and horses two more riders appeared, galloping hard towards him. He raised his gun and fired and they veered off, heading away from the fray. Looking after them, he saw that they weren't the only ones. A number of horsemen were riding back up the slope towards the rocks and he had an intimation that the tide of battle had turned. At the same moment he heard his name being called and he turned to see Eliot ride up.

'Lowell,' he breathed. 'I saw you go off after the breakaways. Are you OK?'

'I'm fine. What about Fuller?'

'Last I saw he was doin' all right.'

'And Lorna?'

Before Eliot could reply there was a fresh salvo of fire. Lowell looked around, expecting Rickard's gunnies to be coming at them again, but the opposite seemed to be the case. All around there were horsemen in retreat, mainly heading up the ridge.

'Come on!' Eliot shouted. 'Looks like we got the varmints on the run!'

He spurred his horse but Lowell did not join him. Instead, he began to ride back to where the chuck-wagon stood at a little distance.

His heart was pounding. Would he find Lorna there? He came up to the wagon and jumped from his horse. Tearing open the canvas, he peered inside. There was a body inside, sprawled face downwards. With fear clutching at his entrails, he climbed in and turned it over. It was one of the gunnies. He crawled forward to the front of the wagon and jumped down. The horses of the remuda had scattered. He couldn't tell whether they had been deliberately loosed or had simply broken free in all the furore. He could see some of them standing forlornly in the driving rain. Back down the line, the sounds of battle had dwindled but he felt no sense of victory. Where was Lorna? He remounted and began to ride, searching desperately for some sign of her.

Suddenly his blood seemed to freeze. Lying on the prairie he saw a body. It could have been any of the Long Rail cowboys. It could have been one of Rickard's hardcases. But he knew it was Lorna. Coming up to the prostrate figure, he jumped down and kneeled beside her. She was lying face down and her rain-lashed body was soaked and streaming, but she was breathing. Very gently he turned her over, holding her head above the swampy ground.

'Lorna!' he breathed.

There was no response and he said it again. This time he felt a shiver go down her body and then her eyes opened.

'The horses,' she said. 'I was trying to bring in some of the horses.'

She was confused but in another moment she recognized him.

'Lowell,' she said, 'Oh Lowell, thank goodness it's you.'

*

From his vantage point high among the rocks, Rickard had been watching the scene with mixed emotions. Things hadn't gone as he planned, but maybe it would turn out OK. He hadn't specifically given orders for his men to attack. It was more a matter of not being able to restrain them. Observing the problems that Fuller and his crew were having with the herd, they had decided the time was ripe to make their move. They were probably right. Certainly Rickard would not have been able to say what was for the best given the unexpected turn that events had taken. So it was that he had decided that the only thing was to make the best of a bad job. His men still had the advantage in terms of numbers. They retained the element of surprise and they were nearly all seasoned gunmen. He was confident of the outcome.

As the struggle proceeded, however, his feelings gradually changed, first to anger and then to anxiety and finally to panic. As he watched more and more of his men break off and ride away, he decided not to wait any longer. The time had come to make his exit. In a state of panic, he made for his horse and, digging his spurs viciously into its flanks, began to make his retreat. His only aim was to get away. He had no idea where he was headed when he saw the mule train in the distance. It was the obvious place to seek refuge. It was his own mule-train and offered an easy way of making it to Shoshone Flats. As he rode down on it he began to feel better. This was just a set-back, a delay, nothing more. He would reorganize and then resume his plans. He carried on riding, not even noticing a rider heading in the opposite direction. It was Conrad, who, having found a suitable spot for the cattle to bed down, was on his way back after hearing the sounds of battle above the crashing of the elements.

The storm began to fade and at last the sky brightened as the men from the Long Rail took stock of the situation. All in all, they hadn't come off so badly. Two men had been killed and others wounded, but they had won the day. The time to try and come to terms with their losses would have to wait. First of all there was the job of rounding up the cattle to be done, and it wasn't going to be easy. As the wrangler hazed in the remuda, the rest of them brought together what cattle they could manage to find in the more immediate area and then, roping fresh horses, they set off to scout the prairie.

The land here was crossed and scarred by run-offs and washes. After the rain the streambeds were bubbling watercourses. The grass had become boggy and the horses found it hard going as their hoofs sank into the marshy ground. The men hadn't gone far, however, before they came upon a number of mangled corpses, the trampled remains of some of Rickard's gunslicks who had been unable to get out of the way of the onrushing herd.

'I guess that's one reason they decided to call it a day,' Fuller remarked.

They found scattered bunches of cattle which they rounded up to bring back to camp, but the bulk of the herd had vanished. Their tracks were easy to follow, but it was a long and wearisome job to reach them, round them up, and drive them back again. By the time the task was completed and the cattle bedded down on the ground Conrad had selected, night had fallen and they were exhausted. Even then, they still weren't quite finished. The front wheels of the chuck-wagon had sunk almost up to the axle and it needed to be righted. Fortunately, the rear wheels were on slightly firmer ground. The cook, with the help of some of the other men, began to unload the wagon in order to make it lighter. Then he blocked the rear wheels, and led one of the horses to the back of the wagon. Fastening a rope to each side of the axle underneath, he slapped the horse across the rump, tugging on the reins and encouraging it to pull. Slowly at first but then with a jolt the wheels came up out of the sodden ground. When it was clear, he re-rigged the horses, returned the jettisoned items and climbed back on the wagon seat. He backed up the wagon, taking care to avoid the marshy patch, and then moved forward again. Only when the operation was completed did he and Lorna between them rustle up some grub for everyone. When they had eaten and downed some strong black coffee, they all felt a little better and gathered closer round the camp-fire to talk things over.

'We'd better not relax our guard,' Conrad said. 'Rickard could be back any time.'

'I don't think so,' Fuller replied. 'I reckon Rickard's shot his bolt. Those gunslicks he hired ain't gonna have any sense of loyalty to him or the Half-Box. I should think they've had enough.'

'I'd be more worried about gettin' the herd across the river,' Conrad remarked. 'It's gonna be swollen with all that rain.'

'What about Rickard himself?' Eliot remarked. 'Did anybody see him?'

There was a general chorus of denial.

'It would be like him to stay out of it,' Fuller said. 'That's his way, to employ others to do his dirty work. He's probably still sittin' pretty back at the

Half-Box M.'

Conrad was thoughtful. 'Hold on a minute,' he said. 'When I heard gunfire and started ridin' back, I saw a man goin' hell for leather in the opposite direction. There was a mule-train out there and I'd say he was headed for it.'

'You reckon it was Rickard?' Fuller said.

'I don't know. It's a fair chance.'

They looked at one another, considering Conrad's words. Lowell downed his coffee and tossed the grounds into the fire.

'I reckon someone should take a look at that mule train,' he said. Fuller turned to him. Even in the flickering firelight Lowell could see the wry look on his face.

'I guess I could spare one man for a spell,' he said.

'I hoped you'd say that,' Lowell replied. 'If Rickard is there, I'll bring him back. Even if he's not, I got a hunch I might just find out where Mossman is anyway.'

Lorna was sitting beside him, none the worse for her experiences.

'You'll be careful, won't you?' she said.

Lowell looked down at her and then at Fuller.

'Don't worry about me,' he said. 'I'll be back before you know it.'

Rickard sat high on a wagon seat at the head of the
mule-train, smoking a cigar. Although he still felt
annoyed about the way things had turned out, his
temper was beginning to improve. Because of cir-
cumstances largely out of his control the attack on
the Long Rail herd had proved abortive, but it
didn't really matter too much. There would be
other opportunities. He cared not a hoot for the
gunslicks who had lost their lives. He had a small
opinion of them and he could always hire more. It
was frustrating but it was nothing more than that.
Now he could supervise the sale of the hides in
person once the mule-train got to Shoshone Flats.
His visit might include a meeting with Mossman.
That would depend on whether he could make
arrangements for Lowell's demise. He was confident that an opportunity would present itself once
Fuller got there with the herd. He toyed with the
idea of carrying it out himself.

It was as he was thinking these things that the
mule-skinner drew his attention to a rider in the
distance. He was moving across the prairie at a considerable speed in their direction. Rickard drew
himself up and stared hard. Who could it be? He
assumed that any of his own men would have

started making their way back to the Half-Box M, but maybe it was one of them. He wished that he had his field-glasses to hand but he had left them in his saddle-bags. As the rider got closer, he began to feel uneasy. There was something familiar about him. Suddenly he turned to the driver.

'Deal with this,' he said. 'Don't let on I'm in the back of the wagon.'

The driver made a grimace in acknowledgement and Rickard slipped inside where he concealed himself behind a pile of provisions. He drew his gun and licked his lips. His throat was dry and his hand trembled. Although a golden opportunity had presented itself, any thought of dealing with Lowell himself now that the man had appeared, vanished from his mind. He had only one thought, and that was to keep out of sight and hope he would go away.

The wagon driver slowed his mules and brought the wagon to a halt as Lowell came up alongside. He was chewing a quid of tobacco and spit a gob of brown juice over the side of the wagon.

'Howdy,' he said.

'Howdy,' Lowell replied. He paused, looking up and down the mule-train.

The smell of the hides hung heavy in the air and further back the flies hung in a dense cloud.

'You kinda lost maybe?' the man said. 'The cow trail is back there.' He jerked a thumb over his shoulder.

'Nope. I've just come from there. I'm lookin', but not for directions.'

The mule-skinner looked at him through hooded eyes. His skin was burned to leather by the sun and he looked like a lizard.

'Shoshone Flats is thataway,' he said, ignoring Lowell's comment and pointing with his finger, 'and Granton is thataway. You might say you're betwixt and between.'

'Like I say, I'm not lookin' for directions. I'm lookin' for someone, a man by name of Rickard.'

The oldster ran his hand across his chin. 'Nope,' he said, 'can't say as I've heard that name.'

Lowell glanced again down the line of wagons and mules. He caught a glimpse of the other drivers. They didn't appear to be taking much interest in the proceedings, but just as he was thinking that a rider appeared from the back of the train and came up alongside.

'We got some kinda problem, Howson?' he asked.

'Nope. Gentleman here is lookin' for someone. Seems to think he might be right here with the mule-train.'

'That's right,' Lowell said. 'A man called Rickard. The name mean anything to you?' The rider shook his head.

'Well, it should,' Lowell said. 'He owns those hides.'

The man exchanged glances with Howson. It was clear to Lowell that they were lying from their response to Rickard's name. At the same time, he suspected that neither of them was anxious to get into an argument.

'Where is he?' Lowell said.

Involuntarily, Howson's eyes flickered towards the interior of the wagon. At the same moment the newcomer's horse shifted its feet and made a sideways movement. Without warning, there was an explosion of gunfire from inside the wagon and the man's horse brayed and toppled over, throwing its rider. Lowell leaped from the saddle and, drawing his weapon, threw himself to the ground. There was another explosion and the mules panicked.

As the driver strove to gain control, Lowell saw a figure leap from the back of the wagon and start to run down the line of wagons on the opposite side. Springing to his feet, he began to run after him. Another shot rang out and though a gap in the line Lowell had a glimpse of legs. He knew that his quarry could only be Rickard. Presumably he was trying to reach his horse at the back of the mule-train. Someone shouted; if it was Rickard calling for assistance, there didn't seem to be any response from the mule-skinners. Lowell hurtled on till he came to a gap between two wagons and slipped through. Not far ahead of him the figure of Rickard plunged on.

'Rickard,' he shouted. 'I've got you covered. You'd better stop.'

There was no response and Lowell fired a shot into the air. Rickard ran on for a few more paces and then came to a halt. He turned and fired the gun he was carrying but the bullet flew harmlessly wide. Lowell began to walk steadily towards him. Rickard's finger squeezed the trigger of his weapon but it only clicked. Desperately, he hurled the useless implement at Lowell and sank to his knees. He began to snivel and plead.

'Please, don't shoot. Please don't shoot. It wasn't me, you can't blame me. Please.'

Lowell stopped in front of the squirming figure of Rickard. It reminded him of Vernon. Behind him, he was aware that a couple of the mule-skinners were standing watching Rickard's grotesque performance with contempt.

'I've only one thing to say to you,' Lowell said.

'Where is Mossman?'

'Mossman? I don't know. I don't know who you mean. Please, don't kill me.' Lowell spun the chamber of his gun.

'One last time,' he said. 'Where is Mossman?'

Rickard's shoulders shook with sobbing. 'He's in Shoshone Flats.'

'Where in Shoshone Flats?'

'He's livin' in a converted rail-car.'

'A rail-car? Why would he do that?'

'I don't know. He owns the railway. He don't like livin' in town. He's, he's. . . .'

'He's what?'

'He don't want to be with people. He likes to keep apart. He keeps movin'.'

Lowell turned to the group which had assembled. 'I'll be takin' Mr Rickard off your hands,' he said. No one raised any objections.

'What are you gonna do with him?' one of the men asked.

'Take him to Shoshone Flats and hand him in to the marshal. Believe me; he's got plenty to answer for.'

CHAPTER SIX

Fuller emerged from the entrance to the frame-constructed Palladium Hotel and glanced up and down the main street of Shoshone Flats. It was a busy place since the arrival of the railroad. People thronged the boardwalks; men on horses and some on mules rode up and down and wagons criss-crossed at the junctions with side streets. At the lower end of the drag a plume of smoke and a general bustle of activity indicated where the new railroad station was situated.

He had just concluded his business with an agent. Earlier that day the herd, which had been left to graze outside the town, had been counted. It had not taken too much time before the final numbers were agreed upon and the delivery sealed. Some of the cattle were sore-footed, but that was hardly surprising. All in all they had come through with remarkably few losses. He was relieved to have them off his hands; they weren't his concern any more.

The only thing to mar his sense of satisfaction was the thought of the lonely graves of the men they had had to bury out on the prairie. His face broke into a frown. The memory made him think of Rickard. It was a tribute to the self-control of his men that they had refrained from taking out their anger on him but had brought him to Shoshone Flats to face justice. Right now he was banged up inside the jail-house awaiting the arrival of the circuit judge. That might take some time, but nobody was shedding any tears.

He was about to turn away when he heard footsteps behind him and turned to see Conrad approaching.

'I'd say we did a good day's business,' he said.

'Yeah. This deal should see us through. I've got a lot to thank you and the men for.'

'I figure we ain't got any reason to stay around.'

'Let the boys let off a little steam for a night or two longer,' Fuller remarked. 'They've earned it.'

Conrad reflected for a moment. 'Yeah, I guess you're right. Me, I figure I'll be stayin' in camp.'

Fuller smiled. He knew his foreman, and it

wasn't his style to look for a good time. He wouldn't be entirely happy till he was in the saddle and on his way back to the Long Rail.

'Come on,' he said. 'I've arranged to meet my niece at the restaurant. She's been doin' some shoppin'. I'll treat you to a pot of coffee.'

'Is she OK goin' around by herself?'

'Why wouldn't she be? She isn't a child.'

'No. I was just thinkin' after what happened. . . .'

'She's fine. Anyway, she's got Lowell along with her.' Fuller looked at his foreman. 'Come on, I don't want to keep her waitin'.'

They strolled down the street to the rather grandly named Elite Restaurant. Inside, sitting at a table near the window, sat Lorna and Lowell. They were deep in conversation and only looked up when Fuller and Conrad were right beside them.

'Oh hello, uncle,' Lorna said. 'And Mr Conrad.'

The newcomers made themselves comfortable and when the waitress arrived, Fuller ordered a fresh pot of coffee for them all. When it came, Fuller poured and they took a few moments to savour it.

'How did you get on with the shoppin'?' Fuller asked.

'Fine. I picked up a few things. I was surprised at the number of stores.'

'That's partly because of the railroad,' Fuller said. 'It wasn't always that way. Lowell might remember it in the old days. Things were a bit different then, eh Lowell?'

Lowell's eyes were on the street and he appeared not to have heard. Lorna glanced at him and he turned back.

'Sorry' he said, 'I was just lookin' at somethin' outside.'

'Yeah? What?' Conrad asked.

'I can't quite make it out. Somethin's goin' on down near the railroad station.' He took another glance and his face broke into a smile.

'Guess what?' he said. 'I think it's Rickard's mule train.'

'Those hides must be gettin' rancid by this time,' Conrad remarked. He turned to Lorna. 'Sorry, ma'am,' he added.

Lorna laughed. 'I should think you're right,' she said.

'It's kind of ironic,' Fuller remarked, 'what with Rickard himself bein' behind bars.'

Lowell twisted in his chair. 'Would anyone object if I go and take a look?' he said. 'I wouldn't mind renewing acquaintance with that old mule-skinner Howson I was tellin' you about.'

'Of course not,' Lorna answered for them all.

'If you're finished here by the time I get back, I'll see you in camp,' Lowell said.

With a smile towards Lorna he got to his feet, made his way out of the restaurant and began walking to the railroad station. There was a considerable amount of activity going on and as he approached he could see that most of it was centred on the mule-train. At the back of the station some cattle pens had been built and the wagons were in process of drawing up nearby. He looked on for a few moments as they manoeuvred, looking for the oldster, but he couldn't immediately see him. In any event it wasn't really the mule train he was interested in. He had made his excuses to leave the table in order to get down to the tracks and look for Mossman's rail car. Rickard had said it was drawn up on a siding so it shouldn't be too difficult to find.

An engine with a carriage attached was standing in the station. He assumed it had come in earlier and deposited its passengers. He began to walk along the roughly constructed platform till, reaching the end, he dropped down on to the cinder track. A little way down was a wooden building with a tin roof. Beside it, on side tracks, an engine stood in an obvious state of disrepair along with a couple of battered boxcars. None of them looked like the sort of thing Mossman would be likely to be living in, but he walked up to each in turn to take a look.

As he surmised, they were empty and awaiting repair. He looked inside the shed but it was empty. He carried on walking a little way and then stopped. He looked down the tracks. There was nothing else to be seen apart from a pile of lumber; just the lines running parallel till they came together and vanished in the distance. He was disappointed. It seemed like Rickard had been lying. Still, it was an unlikely kind of lie. Maybe Mossman had moved on. He considered making another visit to the jailhouse but felt reluctant. He'd had enough of Rickard and didn't relish the prospect of renewing their acquaintance, no matter how briefly.

Yet again Mossman was proving elusive. Suddenly he had a thought. Where were those hides bound for? Who was Rickard dealing with? The obvious answer was that it was Mossman. The two were closely connected in other ways. In general, Rickard seemed to be acting as Mossman's agent in Granton. So maybe the old muleskinner would know where Mossman was to be found. If not, he or somebody else from the mule-train would be dealing with one of Mossman's representatives and the agent might know. Turning on his heel, he began to walk back along the track.

Abbott Mossman's railroad car was not like any other. The windows were frosted glass apart from a larger one at the front end of the carriage, which was of stained glass. It threw a bright, variegated light on to a rich pile carpet and plush-covered furniture with antimacassars, and cushions. Elegant fringed curtains hung at the windows and crystal chandeliers dangled from a painted ceiling. At one end was a cabinet containing bottles of fine wines and spirits, and at the other a leather-topped writing desk and wide easy chair.

On the exterior platform Mossman himself sat drinking a vintage brandy in the shade of the surrounding trees which screened him from the eyes of any inquisitive outsiders. A special section of track had been laid for the car to be shunted into its place of concealment. Mossman himself was as surprising a sight as any of the appurtenances of his special carriage. Lean and bent, with straggling white hair which hung to his shoulders, he gave the impression of someone quite aged, but his smooth features belied it. At the same time there was a strange pallor about his skin, as if it had been bleached. If Lowell or any member of the Long Rail outfit, however, could have seen to whom he was talking, they would have been even more surprised, because it was none other than Rickard.

'Well,' Mossman said in a high piping voice. 'Now that I've arranged for your – what shall we call it? – removal from the jailhouse, I think I may take it that the transfer of the buffalo hides can take place with a minimum of negotiation.'

Lowell nodded. He knew what Mossman meant. He wasn't likely to make any profit on that particular transaction.

'Yes, of course,' he replied.

'And you're quite sure that Lowell has finally been dealt with?'

'Absolutely. You need have no more concerns on that front.'

'Concerns? I wouldn't have put it quite in those terms, but be that as it may. Tell me again; how did you handle it?'

'It was easy enough. A simple ambush.'

'It was meant to be a simple ambush the last time, but it didn't turn out that way.'

'We can all make mistakes. I learned from that episode. No, I can assure you Lowell is dead.'

Rickard was anxious to turn the conversation in a different direction. His rescue from jail on Mossman's initiative hadn't been entirely unexpected, but he had been placed in an awkward situation. The simplest expedient had been to lie. It was highly unlikely that Mossman would come across Lowell in Shoshone Flats and once he was clear of the place, he could make his way back to the Half-Box M and make appropriate arrangements to deal with Lowell once and for all.

'Well,' Mossman said. 'I don't think we need to continue this conversation further.'

Figuratively, Rickard breathed a sigh of relief. Mossman leaned forward and rang a bell which was near his hand. After a few moments, one of his men appeared.

'It's been a pleasure doing business with you,' Mossman said.

He nodded at his man as Rickard rose to his feet, feeling very satisfied the way things had gone. For a few moments he lived in that state of felicity till he found himself staring down the barrel of the gun which the man had just pulled from his pocket. The gun exploded and he sank to his knees, staring in bewilderment. A second shot tore away the top of his head and he fell backwards off the platform to the ground below. Mossman glanced over the rail.

'See that the body is removed,' he said, 'and then make arrangements for the coach to be hitched up to the locomotive. You and the boys can take up an extra carriage. I think it's time for a trip.'

Lowell sought for Howson but couldn't find him. He considered talking with one of the other mule-skinners, but decided Howson was the man to give him the answers he sought. He thought he had a pretty good idea where he might be and made his way to the nearest saloon. He was right. As soon as he walked through the batwings he saw his target lounging against the bar with a bottle of beer in his hand. He sidled up beside him.

'Howdy,' he said. 'How about a shot of whiskey to go with that beer?'

The oldster showed no surprise at seeing Lowell again. Lowell ordered a bottle and invited the man to join him. When they had sat at a table he poured a couple of stiff drinks for them both.

'You made it to town, then,' the oldster conceded after he had taken a few swigs.

'Yeah.'

'Rickard coulda got us killed back there,' Howson said.

'It ain't Rickard I'm interested in anymore,' Lowell said.

A grin spread across the oldster's face.

'Now don't tell me you're lookin' for someone

again,' he said.

'You got it right.'

'Hell, ain't you kinda makin' a habit of this?'

Lowell lifted the bottle and refilled the man's glass. His own stood untouched.

'Guess I am,' he said. 'This time it's someone called Mossman.'

The oldster looked at him closely. If he was surprised, he didn't show it. He seemed to think for a moment before downing another whiskey. Then his face creased into another grin.

'You're too late this time,' he said. 'Mossman pulled out and left town.'

'Left town? When did he do that?'

'About a couple of hours ago. You just missed him. In a manner of speakin', so did I.'

Lowell still hadn't grasped what the man was saying. 'How do you know this?' he said.

'Man at the station.'

'What, you mean he left on a train?'

'You sure catch on,' Howson replied.

Lowell took only a moment to think.

'Thanks, pardner,' he said. 'See you around.'

He got to his feet and began to walk quickly down the smoke-filled room. Howson opened his mouth to shout something after him but before he could speak Lowell had clattered through the batwings and was on his way.

'That man sure has somethin' eatin' him,' Howson mumbled to himself. 'Wonder who he'll be after next?'

With a shrug of his shoulders to all and sundry he poured himself another drink.

Lowell didn't hesitate. He had told Fuller he would be back but there was nothing he could do about that. He had to catch up with Mossman and there was no time to wait. Making his way to the livery stable where he had left his horse, he quickly had it saddled up. He paid the ostler and, leading the sorrel out through the back entrance, climbed into leather. He didn't want to run the chance of any of the others seeing him. There would be explanations, delays, and something else he couldn't put into words, but it concerned Lorna. Most of all, he had the information he needed. He had found Mossman and he didn't mean to let him go. Although Mossman might be travelling fast along his own railroad, he intended to keep riding till he caught up with him.

The horse was well rested and fresh. As soon as he was out of town, Lowell spurred it to a gallop and it stretched out, its mane flowing, following the line of the railroad tracks. He hadn't got far when he saw the added stretch of tracks leading into the grove of trees. He considered taking a closer look but it was pretty obvious that it was where Mossman concealed his railroad car. Even if Mossman had not already left, he would have been unable to see it. The place might be worth examining later, but at present there was no time to spare. Time and speed were of the utmost importance.

Mossman had a good start on him and he didn't know how fast the train was going. For the moment he just let the horse run, but eventually, not wanting it to get blown, he eased it down to a trot, then a walk, then a trot again. After he had been riding that way for a time he topped a low ridge and way off to the north he discerned a black patch moving slowly across the prairie which he surmised was buffalo. He drew to a halt to let the sorrel catch its wind, observing them. He drew out his field-glasses and as he swept the horizon, he saw something else in the distance which quickened his pulse: a faint smudge of what looked like smoke. It might be nothing more than a cloud of dust, but since it lay in the direction of the railroad tracks he was convinced that it was smoke from the stack of an engine. Replacing the binoculars, he touched his spurs to the horse's flanks and urged it once more to a gallop.

He wasn't wrong. As he gradually got closer he became more and more convinced that it was Mossman's train. The rail tracks glistened and the air above them danced in the heat. At times he thought he saw the train ahead of him but each time it proved to be a mirage. Then the smoke seemed to thin and dwindle away. He kept riding as hard as he dared but he could not see it any more. Then he realized that the reason was probably that the train had remained stationary for a while and had moved on again. There was nothing to do but keep going. Then he saw why the train had stopped.

Ahead of him, piled on the prairie, were the black shapes of dead buffaloes. He was reminded of the previous occasion he had found them. These ones had been very recently shot but already the scavengers were busy at their remains. Dense clouds of black flies hung over the scene. Mossman had taken the time for a little sport – except that, as far as Lowell was concerned, it wasn't sport but wanton slaughter. Mossman had not even bothered to get out of the train but just killed them from the security of his railroad car. There was something to be learned, however. From the number of corpses, Lowell reckoned that they couldn't all have been shot by one man. That meant Mossman was not on his own. He had others along with him. How many? There was no way of knowing. He would just have to take his chances – but at least now he was fore-warned.

It was clear to Lowell that he wouldn't catch up with the train unless it stopped again. It was getting late in the day. Since the specialized rail car seemed to be Mossman's home, perhaps the train would halt somewhere for the night. As darkness fell, he kept riding. The sun seemed to pause on the horizon before it dropped over the edge. Night came quite suddenly and starlight glittered like silver on the rails. He was beginning to think he was out of luck when he saw traces of smoke and then, taking him almost by surprise, the looming bulk of the train appeared ahead of him. The loco-motive was pulling two carriages. Light showed at the windows of the rear coach but the one next to the engine was dark apart from the glow of a lantern.

Lowell brought his horse to a halt and dis-mounted. He ground-hitched the animal and then crept up on the train, which was on a siding. Occasionally, muffled voices reached him from the rear coach, but there didn't seem to be much activ-ity. He guessed that Mossman's men were under orders to keep any noise to a minimum. When he reached the rear coach, he carefully peered in at one of the windows. From what he could see, there were half a dozen men inside, sat around a table playing cards. He ducked down and approached the second car. Curtains were drawn at the frosted glass windows and he could see nothing. He moved on. There was no sign of an engineer and he guessed he was probably playing cards with the others. For a moment he hesitated, wondering what to do. Was Mossman inside the car? There was only one way to find out.

Trying to make as little noise as possible, he climbed over the platform rail of Mossman's coach. A lantern was hanging outside the door, casting a warm glow on the stained glass window. Trying to keep out of the radius of its light, he moved to the door and drew his six-gun. He waited for a moment, straining his ears to catch any sound from inside. Hearing nothing, he braced himself and then swung his boot at the door. It flew open and he sprang inside. There was a figure sitting in the semi-darkness. He looked up with a startled expression and then sank back in his chair.

'Mossman!' Lowell snapped.

The tall figure with the lank grey locks seemed to have gathered his composure.

'I am Mossman,' he said. 'But who are you?'

'The name's Lowell, Burt Lowell.'

He had spoken the name very deliberately, but if Mossman was surprised or startled he didn't show it.

'Well, Mr Lowell, I think it only fair to warn you that I have a number of men at my command in the other carriage. I have no idea what your game is, but I can assure you, you have no chance of getting away with anything.'

Lowell's eyes flickered over the carriage, taking in the plush, elaborate fittings.

'On the contrary, I think you might have a very good idea,' he said.

Mossman's eyes, when he looked at Lowell, were blank.

'Why would you think that?' he said.

'Because you've been tryin' to kill me.'

'Trying to kill you? I don't know who you are or what this is about, but I can assure you, if I had reason for wanting to kill you, you would be dead.'

Lowell continued looking about the railroad car.

'Is this why you did it?' he said. 'Is this what it was all for? It's nice, but it doesn't really amount to very much.'

Mossman's mouth opened and he uttered a hollow laugh.

'It's nothing,' he said, 'but it's more than you'll

ever have.'

'I guess that depends on what you're lookin' for.'

'You forget,' Mossman hissed, 'I own the entire railroad company and a lot more besides.'

Lowell grinned. Mossman sat forward and his piping voice, when he spoke, had risen a notch.

'I'd advise you to put that gun down and leave,' he said.

'I wonder how you got your hands on the railroad,' Lowell said. 'Was it the same way you acquired the stagecoach company and the Half-Block M?'

'What business is that of yours?'

'I know you started the fire that burned down Buckhorn. I should. I was marshal there at the time.'

'You were a fool. I gave you due warning.'

'I thought you said you didn't know me.'

'You're still a fool. You come bursting in on me and think you can intimidate me. You throw around wild accusations and question my business activities. Who the hell do you think you are?'

'I think we've already established that you know who I am.' Lowell had a sudden inspiration. 'As for wild accusations,' he said, 'I think you should know that I'm in possession of all the legal papers that were formerly in Dinsdale's safekeeping. Dinsdale, the attorney-at-law back in Granton.'

He looked for a reaction and this time there was one. Mossman's face visibly blanched. It was a long shot, but it had found its mark. He felt pretty certain that, though it might take time and someone with real legal skills to discover it, there would be enough evidence among those papers to destroy Mossman.

'I've had enough of this,' Mossman shrilled.

Lowell hadn't registered the fact that the conversation had risen in tone. In fact, now that he had proven to his satisfaction that his suspicions about Mossman were true, he felt somewhat at a loss as to how to proceed. Since learning that Mossman had left on his private train, he had been acting more or less from instinct. The whole situation seemed strangely unreal. Although Mossman had lost something of his *savoir faire*, he didn't appear to be unduly alarmed by Lowell or his six-gun. Was he being brave? Lowell suspected that it was more to do with his overweening arrogance. He had come to consider himself outside the common run – immune and invincible.

Mossman made to get to his feet and at the same moment Lowell heard a sound of movement coming from the roof of the train. He glanced up and for the first time noticed a skylight across which a dark shadow had fallen. In the same instant that he knew there was somebody on the roof he squeezed the trigger of his six-gun. The glass shattered and there was a loud scream. He heard a noise behind him and swinging round, fired again through the open door of the carriage. He heard an almost plaintive moan and then a thud as somebody collapsed on the outside platform of the car. Lowell sprang to the door and as the man attempted to rise, swung his boot and caught him on the tip of his chin. He heard a snap and the man went limp. He was under attack and he didn't know how many of them there were. As stabs of flame lit the night and lead flew past, he took a leaf from the rooftop gunman's book and, climbing on to the rail, heaved himself up to the roof of the train. Bullets were whining and singing as they ricocheted from the metal of the locomotive. A shot from close below whistled past his cheek. He looked down and in the light of the rear carriage window he had a clear view of two men by the side of the track. Before either of them could fire again, he let loose with his six-gun. One man fell and the other staggered back as his own gun exploded harmlessly into the ground. Lowell fired again and the man collapsed, disappearing from his line of vision.

The sequence of shots was followed by silence. Lowell lay along the roof of the train, listening for any tell-tale sounds which might give away the presence of more attackers. He had seen six of Mossman's men through the window of the train and he had accounted for four of them. There might have been more, but he didn't think so. The man he had shot through the skylight lay on his back nearby, his empty eyes staring at the heavens. Lowell jammed slugs into the chamber of his gun and then, reaching out with his foot, pushed the corpse over the side of the train. It fell with a dull thump and as Lowell had hoped, one of the gunnies opened fire. This time it came from inside the car and Lowell was pretty sure that those of Mossman's guards who remained were still in there. If so, he might be able to take them by surprise if he assumed the initiative.

Slowly, he raised himself up and had just begun to move when there was a blinding flash of light and the loud report of a rifle. He felt a searing pain in his leg as the blast sent him toppling over the side of the train. For what seemed a long period of time he felt himself falling through space till his fall was arrested by a savage jolt and for a moment he lay winded and semi-conscious. He was sufficiently aware of the gravity of his situation, however, to roll underneath the train. As he did so a pair of legs appeared on the opposite side. He couldn't afford to take the slightest chance so he raised his gun and blasted away. There was a howl of anguish and the man fell. His head appeared on a level with Lowell's, twisted in agony. His rifle lay just beyond and they both reached out to take it. Lowell, however, was restricted by the train's undercarriage and the wounded man's hand got to it first. Grimacing with pain, he strove to bring it round. Lowell's leg was hurting but the first initial shock of pain had ceased and he was still mobile. Rolling away, he got clear just as the rifle exploded.

The shot whined, ricocheting from a wheel, and as the man fired again, Lowell hobbled round the end of the train and came up behind him. The man lay like a snake with its back broken, at his mercy. He tried in vain to raise the rifle and looked up at him with pleading eyes. Lowell stamped on his hand to release the man's grip and picked up the rifle. He stood panting for a few moments, listening. He could hear sounds of movement near the engine and began to move away towards the back of the train. He rounded the carriage and stood erect, supporting himself against it. How many of the gunnies were left? Only one? He peered cautiously round the side of the car but could see nothing. The sound of voices reached his ears and he tried to ascertain how many people were involved. Then one of the voices rose higher and he recognized the thin tones of Mossman.

'What the hell do you mean?' he was shouting, 'you don't know where he is?'

Another voice murmured something in reply and then Mossman's whining vibrato shrilled again.

'He can't be far! Go and find him!'

The man Lowell had shot in the leg lay moaning, adding his sounds to those of the others. Lowell stepped back and tried to think. It was hard to keep a clear head. Should he try and make it to his horse? The night had grown dark as clouds scudded overhead. The track was veiled in shadow. He would probably have been able to make it if it wasn't for his damaged leg. He looked over the silent, empty prairie and thought he heard a distant rumble. Sounds carried far. It could be a herd of buffalo. The sound faded and he thought he must have been mistaken. He couldn't afford to give it any attention because there was at least one more gunnie left.

He listened for footsteps but his ears only picked up the rumbling sound again. He hadn't been mistaken. Something was causing it. Could it be horsemen? Who would be riding at that time of night? If it was caused by horsemen, there must be a sizeable group of them. Suddenly he saw a point of light. Despite his perilous situation, he watched in a kind of fascination as it grew and got nearer, like the eye of some ravening Cyclops.

He still couldn't work out what it was but as the rail beneath his feet began to vibrate he suddenly realized it was a train. The rumbling swelled to a roar and he could see sparks fly from its smoke-stack. It drew on, and as it got closer he perceived that it comprised only an engine with its caboose. At the same moment two figures emerged from the side of the car behind which he was pressed. He raised the rifle to take a shot but decided against it. The night was too dark and the likely outcome would simply be to give his position away. He lowered the weapon and shrank further into the frame of the carriage as the two men carried on moving till they were soon lost to sight. Lowell real-ized he was in a real fix. One of the figures was Mossman and the train could only be carrying more of his men.

The engine was almost upon him now and the noise it made resounded like thunder. A light appeared and began to move backward and forward. It was Mossman waving a lantern.

Suddenly Lowell could see his lank shape outlined against the beam thrown by the headlights of the train. Involuntarily, he started forward. What was Mossman doing? Lowell could not see clearly, but he seemed to have stepped on the track right in the path of the train.

The engine plunged on and then, even above its deafening roar, Lowell heard a tremendous scream which seemed to split the night and sent a shiver of dread down his spine. The light of the lantern disappeared. There was a loud hissing of steam and the screech of iron upon iron as the engine driver applied the brakes. Sparks flew as the engine rolled and rattled and slid past the siding. Lowell watched in stunned horror. What had Mossman been thinking of? He could only assume he had meant to send a signal to the driver to stop, but what had taken possession of him to take such a risk? He had probably grown desperate as the number of his guards depleted. Whatever the answer, Mossman was now just a mangled, squashed piece of blood and bone on the track. What had happened to the other man?

The engine slowed at last and then came to a grinding halt. Lowell was jerked back to life. At any moment Mossman's men were about to pile out of the caboose. He hefted the rifle, ready to sell his life dearly, and leaned out again to see what was happening. Men were getting out of the caboose and moving cautiously towards Mossman's train. It was hard to make things out but something about them puzzled him. He had expected them to come out whooping and shouting, looking for trouble. These men were acting in just the opposite fashion, being very circumspect. Did they realize what had happened? They came closer, four of them, and then suddenly his heart thumped and a wave of relief began to flow over him. He recognized them now. They weren't more of Mossman's gunslicks. It was Fuller, Eliot and Conrad, and the person with them, who it took a few more moments for him to recognize, was the oldster, Howson.

Stepping out into the open, Lowell waved his arms and shouted, 'It's me, Lowell! Hell, I'm sure glad to see you boys!'

By way of reply a gunshot rang out behind him and a bullet thudded into the wood of the rail car near his head. It was met by a hail of fire from Fuller and Conrad. There was the sound of a groan as someone hit the ground. He knew he had been careless to ignore the last gunman. He also knew now what had become of him. He limped forward, throwing the rifle aside, as Eliot came to his assistance.

'Are you hit bad?' he said.

'I don't think so.'

He would have collapsed but Eliot and Howson between them lowered him to the ground.

'Are there any more of the varmints?' Fuller called.

'I don't think so, but you'd better check out the train.'

While Fuller and Conrad were carrying out a search of the train, Eliot was doing the best he could to treat Lowell's injury. As Lowell had surmised, it was a flesh wound. A bullet had gone through his calf. He had lost a considerable amount of blood but Eliot effectively stemmed the flow, using their bandanas as a temporary bandage and tourniquet.

'This seems familiar,' he commented. 'Man, you're pushin' your luck.'

Just as he was finishing, Fuller and Conrad returned.

'You're a damn fool,' Fuller said. 'You should have took us along with you in the first place.'

Lowell summoned up a grin. 'I guess you're right,' he said, 'but then it was kinda personal.' He lay back, looking up into their faces. 'Oh yes. By the way, since when did any of you learn to drive a train?'

Fuller pointed to Howson. 'He's your man,' he said. 'Seems like he's been an engineer in his time.'

Just then the engine they had come in gave a loud noise and a fresh burst of steam began to hiss and boil.

'Leastways, that's what he says.'

Howson spat a gob of brown liquid through his front teeth.

'I got you here, didn't I? Me and that old engine between us.'

'I'm glad you did,' Lowell said. 'Things weren't lookin' too good there for a while.'

Fuller glanced dubiously at Howson and then at the engine. 'Hell,' he said, 'You and that loco between you have got to get us all back again yet.'

Lowell lay on the floor of the caboose smoking a cigarette. Conrad had taken charge of his horse and was riding it back to Shoshone Flats. Beside him, Fuller sat with his back to the wall while, at a little distance, the injured gunslick sprawled unconscious, still clutching a bottle of medicine in his hand. It was something Howson had produced and it contained rot-gut whiskey laced with morphine. The oldster himself was grappling with the engine, with Eliot's help. As it rattled along the track, the whole contraption shook and heaved.

157

Every now and then it gave a lurch and smoke and steam found its way through the cracks and crevices of the car. Ahead of the heaving engine the headlights, like a scimitar, sliced through the darkness with their sharp beam of light.

'I got everythin' to thank you boys for,' Lowell said.

'You certainly cut it fine this time,' Fuller replied.

'I don't mean just that. No, it's somethin' more. I don't know how to put it. I feel as though somethin's changed. I feel kinda different. Whatever it is, I owe it to you all.'

'You've been alone too long,' Fuller replied. 'It ain't good for a man.'

Lowell took a pull on his cigarette. 'How did you find out I'd gone after Mossman?'

'One of the boys, Tremlow, saw you talkin' with Howson. When you suddenly shot out of that saloon, he figured there was somethin' up and had a word with the oldster. Hell, you've been makin' a regular habit of landin' yourself in trouble.'

'And you've all been makin' a habit of gettin' me out of it again.'

Fuller seemed to consider the matter. 'Yeah,' he concluded, 'I guess there's a kind of pattern. It was Howson's idea to take the old engine. He reckoned it would save a lot of time, but the trouble it took to get it goin', I'm not so sure. I figure he never had any liking for Mossman either.'

Lowell hesitated for a moment. 'What about Lorna?' he said, trying to make the question sound neutral.

'She's fine. Tremlow rode with her back to the camp.'

'I expect she'll be worried.'

Fuller gave him a quizzical look. 'Yeah, I guess so. We told her a story but I suppose she'll see right through it.'

There was another lurch and then the train continued its way.

'You're welcome to stay at the Long Rail just as long as you want,' Fuller said. 'I take it you weren't intendin' goin' back to that ghost town?'

Lowell shook his head. 'Thanks,' he replied, 'I'll take you up on that offer.'

'Welcome back,' Fuller said. Lowell wasn't quite sure what he meant, but it sounded good. 'Once we're back at Shoshone Flats, I figure takin' a day or two to rest up and let the boys blow their money, if they haven't done it already. Then we'll start headin' back for the Long Rail. One way and another, it's been quite a ride.'

Lowell took another drag of the cigarette and

very gingerly stretched his injured leg.

'Yeah,' he said, taking up Fuller's own expression. 'It'll be good to be back again.'